At the Crossroads:
A Southern Daughter's Story

Jean Gottlieb Bradley

Sale of this book without a cover may be unauthorized. If this book is coverless it may have been reported to the publisher as destroyed or unsold. Neither the author nor publisher may have received payment for it.

At the Crossroads:
A Southern Daughter's Story
is based on some true stories, but the characters are a composite of many people. Any references to actual persons, historical events, or real locales are used fictitiously.

At the Crossroads:
A Southern Daughter's Story

Copyright © 2014 by Jean Gottlieb Bradley
First Edition 2015

ISBN 978-0-9906125-0-6

Published by
Mont View Press

montviewpress.com

All Rights Reserved
Reserved rights include the right of reproduction in whole or in part in any form.

Cover painting: **At the Crossroads**
Artist: Patrick John Daugherty
Copyright © 1999, Patrick John Daugherty
All Rights Reserved

Je schoener und voller die Erinnerungen desto schwerer ist die Trauer. Aber die Dankbarkeit verwandelt die Erinnerung in eine stille Freude.
Man traegt das vergangene Schoene nicht wie ein Stachel, sondern wie ein kostbares Geschenk in sich.

The richer and more beautiful the Remembrance, the harder is the Sorrow, but the Thankfulness turns the Remembrance into a quiet Joy.
One should not carry the past Beauty as a Thorn, rather as a treasured Gift within.

Dietrich Bonhoeffer, (1906-1945)

Dedicated to the incredible Braun family with love.

Contents

CHAPTER ONE
The Farm 1

CHAPTER TWO
Savannah 24

CHAPTER THREE
The Mormons 47

CHAPTER FOUR
Poetry 66

CHAPTER FIVE
Medical School 79

CHAPTER SIX
Remembering Dad 91

CHAPTER SEVEN
Family Struggles 105

CHAPTER EIGHT
Leaving Georgia 128

CHAPTER NINE
Fate of Innocents 147

CHAPTER TEN
Recovering 159

CHAPTER ELEVEN
Jurisprudence 172

CHAPTER TWELVE
In the Himalayas 186

Epilogue 207

Acknowledgements

Many people gave the generous gift of time by reading early drafts, asking questions and offering advice. I would like to thank "test readers" Carolyn Saradar, Beatrice Hook, Ernst Jung, Sue White, Margarete Laier, Reinhold Braun, Henry Emilsson, and those in my family who gave tireless time and encouragement. Special thanks goes to Doris Coldren who helped me organize my chapters and who also gave many excellent tips.

Ellen and her husband Patrick Daugherty were pivotal people in bringing the book to fruition. Ellen, a writer's dream editor, was always enthusiastic, patient and persistent as we worked through various passages. Patrick is an artist extraordinaire, and contributed with his technical support and organizational skills. This book would not have been possible without their encouragement and talents. I am forever in their debt.

Letter from the Author

Dear Reader,

This is my first novel and it has been a roller coaster ride. It is based on many true stories; only the names have been changed to protect the innocent. What inspired me was all the wonderful people I have come to know during my lifetime and I felt the need to capture their unique qualities through this novel.

I have been an archivist of old letters for many decades. In an electronic age, society often forgets about the hand-written letters that we older people waited feverishly to receive. In addition to personal correspondence, I have been a regular collector from flea markets and antique shops of old photos and letters from the 19th and 20th centuries.

This novel has been a labor of love; the letters provide a backbone and are interwoven in the story. They give some insight into the personalities and struggles of my characters. The content of the correspondence was left unchanged.

It is a story of two families, the Johnsons and the Blaskeys. The Johnsons were fourth generation farmers, but insecure about their positions in life because they could not easily embrace people and cultures that were foreign to them.

The Blaskeys lived seemingly unselfish lives because they were secure in their love for each other and the world around them. They were fourth generation Christian missionaries.

Because the book spans several decades from the '50s through the '70s the influences of segregation, Jim Crow, and the Ku Klux Klan are also part of the story.

It is a story not only about healing through faith, adventure, forgiveness, and redemption, but also about overcoming tragic loss through love.

I hope this novel will give you a window into a period of time that can so easily be forgotten.

My very best wishes,

Jean Gottlieb Bradley

Kindness is the golden chain by which society is bound together.

       Johann Wolfgang von Goethe

Chapter One
The Farm

I grew up in middle Georgia where there were some rolling hills and lots of pine trees. In the 1950's, there were still quite a few stands of longleaf pines that can grow, if undisturbed, for hundreds of years. Economically it was a poor area with a lot of natural beauty. The longleaf pines had long branches so the trees in the forest were well spaced and not crowded. Today there are tree farms with faster growing varieties of trees yielding lots of pine needles used for mulch and timber used for fence posts and paper pulp; the trees are planted quite close to each other for these cash crops. In the latter half of the 20th century, the longleaf pine became over harvested, so the USDA (United States Department of Agriculture) began promoting subsidy programs to encourage the replanting of this type of tree, which gives rise to a more diverse habitat for plants and animals.

As a child, I loved to walk in the woods along the paths that the domestic and wild animals had forged years before I arrived. It was a peaceful environment in which to think and relax, especially by a small stream that ran through the property. There were some wild magnolia trees thriving near this stream, and they gave a wonderful fragrance to the air. As the wind whispered through the pines, it brought a lovely sense of calm to my heart. So many birds called out to each other with their sweet melodies for all to hear within earshot. Later in the evening, the wanderer could hear the whippoorwills contacting one another. I felt a kinship with the land.

The soil was a combination of sand and humus, which was good for growing trees and "wiregrass" which is a tan to golden bunchgrass that grows calf-high. This grass was often harvested by the tenant farmers and made into brooms for sweeping the yard. Debris was not allowed to accumulate. Even the smallest house in the country always had a well-swept yard. Pecan trees were often planted around houses in the South and they were dirty trees with falling blossoms in the spring and the husks from the nuts in the fall. However, sweeping the yards made it easier to gather the pecans, and a clean yard was a source of satisfaction as well as pride.

My mother was a teacher and my father did some truck farming after they were married. I was born seven years later, and since they were both quite busy I was mostly left in the hands of my grandmother for childcare. My grandmother had inherited the farm from her father, my great grandfather. Since she was divorced and had two children, it gave her a measure of security. Her other siblings had been compensated and they were grateful that she stayed behind to look after their elderly father. My grandmother always had a big garden so that our food supply came basically from what we planted and harvested. We always had a bountiful crop of fresh vegetables.

The farm was located at the Crossroads, which was justly named, because it was located at the intersection of two highways. At the turn of the 20th century, my Great Grandpa Holsworth had owned all four corners of the junction, but by the time of my birth, the four corners were owned by three different families—my family possessed two.

My dad was industrious and enterprising in buying and selling. His customers really liked him. Even though he controlled his anger with them, he had a problem with anger management and it often was directed at my mother. As a little girl I was not affected by this side of him, only later in life did I experience it.

My earliest childhood memories involve the Nehms family. This family was an integral part of our lives even though they were tenant farmers, who helped plant and bring in the crops. Tenant farming was a common practice in Georgia and our farm was no exception. The Rodney Nehms family, who helped, came to live at the Crossroads when I was four years old.

The Nehms were a large family with seven children and lived up the hill from us in the old farm house which had been built by Walter Holsworth, my great grandfather, when he first moved from North Carolina to Georgia, in the late 1890's. The Nehms family consisted of Rodney, Ellie Mae his wife, and daughters Marie, Betsey and youngest son, Derek. The older children had left home before their family moved to our place. They became my second family and I bonded easily with them.

Laurie Mae was born out of wedlock to Marie. Her father treated her harshly when he found out she was pregnant and may even have beaten her. After her daughter was born, Marie left the farm, but her baby, Laurie, remained with Ellie Mae and Rodney, who became principals in her rearing. She was named after my grandmother Laurie Parker and her grandmother, Ellie Mae.

Marie moved to Savannah, where she was hired by one of the hospitals to work in the kitchen. Like her mother, Marie was a good cook, but she still visited the farm, so Laurie would know that she was her mom. I was about four years old when Laurie was born. When she was older we often played together and we loved to go to each other's houses for visits as well. The older girls, who were Laurie's aunts, liked to comb and braid my hair. It never took too much persuasion for me to submit to the soft strokes of their brushes and combs. There was not a braided hairstyle those aunts didn't try on me while they so affectionately stroked my hair. I loved them, and my mom and I always shopped for them at Christmas to show my gratitude.

Several of the older children moved to Florida, settling around Sanford where the oldest brother lived. Their work was mostly labor, probably working on the vegetable truck farms in that area of central Florida during the 50's. One of the oldest girls eventually headed north for Detroit.

Blacks and Whites went to separate schools during our American apartheid, and while they were living on the farm, Betsey and Derek both finished the twelfth grade at the Black high school, eventually gaining good employment.

I was aware of segregation, but, sadly, it was so culturally accepted within the South we seldom questioned its morality. Our two families got along and helped each other in various ways. Betsey wanted to go to the senior prom; she was really ecstatic when Mother gave her an apricot chiffon calf-length dress I had worn to several parties and dances. Years later, she visited me in Pennsylvania with Laurie, and I heard that she had a successful career with the telephone company with an excellent severance package. The two of them just showed up one day at my office; it was a fabulous reunion.

After finishing college, Laurie taught school for my Uncle Earl in a coastal community where he was the county school superintendent. She later married the fireman detective, Leonard, whom she began dating while teaching. During the 1970's, my uncle shared the story of how Laurie and her husband were the first Blacks that he had ever invited to his home for dinner. This was a significant event in the Deep South—a milestone in racial relations. Laurie was family!

Uncle Earl's office, as county school superintendent, was an elected political position. During the '60s and early '70s, he had to tread gently so as not to offend anyone. Most of the time he ran unopposed, but during his last elections the National Association for the Advancement of Colored People (NAACP) unsuccessfully tried to provide him with some opposition. Having Laurie on his side certainly did not harm his chances for winning re-elections as county superintendent.

On the farm one of the annual events the Rodney Nehms were always a part of was hog-killing time. As gruesome as it seemed to me, I loved this time. Our families worked together, so harmoniously. No harsh words were ever spoken, and there was always a flurry of things to do that was accompanied by plenty of laughter. Large cauldrons of water boiled over on open fire. Rodney killed the hogs and then they were hung up on a large branch of the big pecan tree. After the hot, scalding water was poured over the skin, he shaved the hogs as slick as he could. We had a smoke house where the shoulders and hindquarters were smoked with hickory wood, heavily salted and hung from the rafters to finish the curing process. The hams were preserved much like beef jerky is today. Refrigeration had not yet come into its own.

After most of the blood had been drained from their bodies, the hogs were disemboweled and the intestines were cleaned. This delicacy was called chitlings and most Blacks, as well as some Whites, loved to eat them. We seldom ate chitlings, but the Rodney Nehms loved them. I don't remember exactly what the arrangement for dividing up the meat from the pig was, but I always had the feeling my family was fair. Ellie Mae knew how to speak up, if she thought it necessary. She was a self-assured Negro woman and willing to speak her mind.

Hardly anything was wasted; the pig's skin was cut up and fried to make cracklings that were used to make a hardy cornbread. Then the lard was rendered and used in baking. Various left over pieces of meat that were hardly recognizable, such as tongue and the head of the pig, were used to make "press meat" that rivaled the best French pate.

The part of the pork I loved to eat most was the sausage. Mom, my grandmother, and Ellie Mae knew just the right amounts of sage, salt and pepper, and a dash of thyme for seasoning—the taste of the sage is what stayed with me over the years. Seasoning sausage is an art and I have not eaten any since my childhood that tasted quite as good. Seasoning takes time and experimentation, tasting and stirring, and mixing and re-sampling; not many people allow themselves to take that much time. Nowadays nearly everything we buy is corporately grown, processed, packaged, and distributed. Most people cannot identify from what part of the pig or cow the various cuts of meats originate.

Around the age of five, my family decided to build a new house at the farm. When our home was ready, the Nehms family moved into our old house, where we had lived without indoor plumbing. Prior to this move they had been living a short distance from the farm. Our new quarters had indoor plumbing, but it definitely was not an affluent dwelling. At the same time in a poor county, it was quite respectable. Timber from the farm was cut and used for its framing. Some of the rooms were entirely built out of pine boards. The house sat among a grove of pecan trees and the nuts were gathered by everybody in the late fall and early winter. This was a task I did not enjoy. It was sandy and dirty and we had no fancy equipment to gather the individual nuts.

Our new white, framed house had four bedrooms, a parlor, dining room, and a huge eat-in country kitchen. My grandmother kept her woodstove for cooking because electricity was not always reliable, but we also had an electric range and the kitchen was up to date for 1949 standards. A huge chest freezer was kept in the kitchen and my family was always "putting up" for later use. For instance, we were generous with all the relatives when they came for visits, especially Uncle Earl, my mother's brother.

With rural electricity, we had frequent power outages during thunderstorms. The wood stove and my grandmother's kerosene lamps were welcome backups. Even as a thunderstorm raged outside, I felt safe and protected as we huddled together around the lamp and I listened to the adult conversations. We often went to bed in the dark and discovered we had electricity the following morning. Everyone had a flashlight by his bedside.

Sometimes we took the vegetables from the farm to the school cafeteria, where we had access to the large cooking vats and a small canning plant. The foodstuff was packed in pint and quart-sized metal containers and then turned over for processing to the person in charge of the canning operation. We usually picked up the finished cans a few weeks later and shared them with the Nehms and various relatives when they visited. This canning process was a wonderful way of utilizing county equipment in the schools during the summer vacation. Otherwise, everything would have been idle. This was a great benefit to the farming community in a poor county.

Our country store was built in 1950 and a few years after that the Rodney Nehms got a new house on the farm with indoor plumbing. My family knew an excellent brick mason and he was kept busy with expansion projects. It was a modest white blockhouse with a living room, dining room, two bedrooms and a small front porch. By this time only Mae, Rodney and Mr. Walt, Ellie Mae's stepfather lived in the house but had extended summer visits from grandchildren. The Nehms were an essential part of our lives for over 20 years. Throughout high school, college and part of medical school, we were interwoven in each other's lives.

In college, I majored in chemistry and experimented with making beer. A fellow chemistry major had given me a list of what to get. My bedroom at the farm smelled like a brewery, which it was. Well, Mr. Walt was my biggest partaker. Several times I offered him some quart jars of beer. He loved it and would sit on his front porch to drink it.

"Ms Joan, you got any more of that beer?" he often asked. Then I would take him a few more quarts. The two of us were the sole consumers. About the only thing that can be said of my efforts, is that it tasted like beer. But not having had much experience in making or drinking it; this was my first try as a "brew master." Luckily, I had a pleased patron.

During the visit from Laurie and Betsey in the '90s, while we were living in Pennsylvania, we had a lot of reminiscing to do and traded stories of our childhood. At one point in our reminiscing Laurie told me, "I used to think you had it so good!" I replied without hesitation,

"Looks can be deceiving!"

Sometimes I wondered if my mother really loved me because of some of the bizarre things she did during my formative years. She scared me with all sorts of critters and encouraged me to play with frogs! Mother often laughed about my fear of harmless creatures. The "creepy crawlies" created a phobia, but I finally learned to be bold and could pick up frogs and worms; however, the horned caterpillars found on tomato plants still scared me. There is little question, she probably had been terrorized as a child herself, and this was learned behavior.

My fear of worms probably also came from listening to the morbid talks my grandmother gave on the subject of insects and worms devouring the bodies of the dead. My father's dad, a "hard shell Baptist," often talked the same morbid way. Mama Parker often told me that after she died, she would try and come back to me—I didn't know whether to be scared or to look forward to this reunion.

As a youngster, I worked with the farm hands, "handing" green tobacco. I was an eager learner and wanted to do everything that my "Black sisters" were doing. The tobacco left an awful sticky mess on our hands and it was hard to wash off, even with the harshest soap and water. After the tobacco leaves were tied with string on a wooden pole, it was "cured" in a huge barn with propane gas heaters until it turned a golden brown. I also picked cotton with some of the older girls. I wanted to know everything.

My experience with cotton wasn't as good as with tobacco. Working in the cotton field, in the heat of the sun, was more tedious work, requiring more concentration. It was really a backbreaking job that also gave the cotton picker sore fingers. Today machines do this work. "Handing" green tobacco was more of a social event, where there was plenty of conversation, peppered with laughter, under the shelter of an open-air barn.

After the drying process, the tobacco was removed and layered in large burlap bales to be taken to market. In the huge warehouse, there was an auction wherein the biggest cigarette and cigar buyers would bid on the different farmer's tobacco. In order to get a good price, my mother preferred that I stand on the burlap bales. By standing on the tobacco, I let the buyer, she had spoken to earlier, know where ours was located in this large building, thereby giving us a better price for the crop. At the time I was seven or eight—old enough to feel conspicuous. It was very humiliating for me to have to do, but nevertheless I complied. Reflecting on it, those episodes seemed cheap and degrading—a pathetic, ridiculous request to make of a small child. Laurie, Betsey and I had heartfelt exchanges.

The girls were especially grateful that my mom had paid into the Social Security Benefit Program for Ellie Mae, thereby assuring her of a small pension later in life. Since my mother was a teacher, she was knowledgeable about such matters. Our whole family shared its fondness for the Nehms, especially Ellie Mae.

Laurie told me an interesting story about a shopping trip she had made with my mom in a nearby town. She was the apple of my mother's eye and often traveled with her. Laurie was always on the farm during the summers, and in her early years she had lived with Ellie Mae and Rodney most of the time. While they were shopping in one of the stores, Laurie needed to urinate. Mother asked Mr. Seaman where the bathroom was and explained the little girl needed to use the toilet. He replied there were no facilities for Negroes. Beatrice, my mother, looked at Laurie and said,

> "Well, Laurie, go ahead and just piss right here in the store!"

Needless to say, he showed her to the bathroom real quick. This must have happened during the late '50s. There was great admiration in Laurie's voice as she told this story. I know she loved my mom dearly for standing up to the shop keeper and allowing her to use the toilet. She followed my mom into the teaching profession and enjoyed a successful career.

"Separate, but equal," became commonplace in the South. We were living during the Jim Crow era. There are lies, and then there are damn lies; that may be a good summary of how these laws came about. The origin of the phrase Jim Crow has been attributed to "Jump Jim Crow", a song and dance caricature of Blacks, originally performed by white actor Thomas Rice in blackface. Originating in the 1830's, it became a pejorative term for Negroes. In the later part of the

19th century, when southern legislatures passed segregation laws, they became known as Jim Crow laws. Segregation even carried over to the military and federal workplaces into the middle part of the 20th century, until President Harry Truman desegregated the military.

The White people and the Black people had gotten along well together, but suddenly they became suspicious and cautious of one another. The "outhouses" were becoming a thing of the past, and more and more public facilities had indoor toilets and drinking fountains. Almost overnight, each race had to have separate bathrooms and drinking fountains.

Sexually transmitted diseases were rampant among both races, and rumors got around that you could catch them from toilet seats. This led to even more discrimination, and worries about the diseases Blacks might pass on to Whites.

Penicillin was not discovered until the 1940's and this was a cure for most sexually transmitted diseases from which Blacks and Whites both suffered. Such sexually transmitted diseases as syphilis and gonorrhea were prevalent and syphilis affected the vascular and nervous systems in its advanced stages. People during the 20th century and probably to this day think that a lot of diseases can be caught if a person sits on the toilet seat. Prior to Penicillin, syphilis was treated with heavy metals and the cure could be quite painful. Later in medical school I was told, if you want to understand what a disease can do to the body, study syphilis—there is hardly any organ of the body that it doesn't affect. It can be a devastating disease.

I learned more about the diseases as I advanced in medical school. Primary syphilis starts with a sore on the penis or within the vagina, and if untreated, becomes secondary syphilis with a widespread generalized rash involving the palms and the soles. Tertiary syphilis manifested itself in the joints, nervous system and cardiovascular system.

My studies disclosed that an interesting experiment was conducted on syphilis starting in the 1930's. The Tuskegee Institute, located in Alabama, became part of the syphilis experiment in 1932. Booker T Washington, one of the South's most accomplished Negroes, founded the Tuskegee Institute with the help of northern philanthropists including Julius Rosenwald (President of Sears, Roebuck and Company). The Tuskegee Institute was like the Harvard of the South, in developing schools, small businesses and research, especially its agricultural research on the peanut.

In 1926, syphilis was seen as a major health problem with prevalence of 35% in the reproductive population. Aggressive treatment during the 1920's had less than a 30% cure rate with bismuth, mercury and neoarsphenamine (derived from arsenic) being the treatment of choice.

For 40 years between 1932 and 1972 the U S Public Health Service conducted experiments on 399 men with syphilis and 201 without. The Black men did not receive proper informed consent but were told they would get treatment for "bad blood," a colloquial term used to describe fatigue, anemia, and syphilis. They only knew the disease sapped them of all their energy.

Even when I was in residency in the early '70s, one of the questions I was taught to ask black men was, "Have you ever been treated for bad blood?" In the study most of the men were illiterate sharecroppers from poor counties in Alabama. The doctors knew they would not get the high dosages of heavy metals because the experiment was designed to acquire the final results by postmortem autopsies. Most of the men received the pink medicine—aspirin. They were left to degenerate under the ravages of tertiary syphilis that included heart disease, blindness, and insanity—thereby showing the natural course of a disease if left untreated.

Many educated African Americans collaborated with the white government officials who ran the experiment and they were their trusted advisors. Most likely the Tuskegee Institute hoped to gain more prestige from its association with the U.S. Public Health Service.

Penicillin finally became the drug of choice in 1945, and proved to cure the disease; however, penicillin was not offered to the African American men and the experiment continued with the support from the American Medical Association and the Negro Medical Association chapters as late as 1969. In 1974, a class action suit provided some financial and health benefits to the participants. James Jones extensively studied the Tuskegee Experiment, and he identified the study as "the longest non-therapeutic experiment on human beings in medical history." Jones' book, *Bad Blood: The Tuskegee Syphilis Experiment*, published in 1993, was an eye-opening analysis of how research was conducted on these black men.

Many of these separate facilities for Blacks persisted into the early '70s. The signs designated where colored people should drink, go to the toilet and other signs stated, "We serve colored with carry out only." Serving "colored" came to include Mexicans and Indians as well.

Whoever started this fallacy did a great job of selling it to the public. It may have grown out of the Ku Klux Klan ideology of White supremacy, and the resentment which they felt toward black Americans, who were a reminder of the Confederacy's loss of the Civil War. As a child of five or six, I saw a cross burning, but it was not at a black family's house. It was a poor white family that lived down by the river; the man in this family was being singled out for not providing adequate care for his family.

Today, we have people who have conjured other ways of showing their holiness and support for their Christian principles. The Ku Klux Klan around our rural community was more of a religious-vigilante group that swung their weight when Christian laws were broken. I was really too young to understand everything. In retrospect, this person was white and not the stereotypical Negro, who was being harassed. At the time it was to send a message of "Shape up or there will be consequences." For example, if a husband was beating his wife and didn't shape up, his next encounter might be a flogging instead of a cross burning. The KKK in some southern communities seemed like the police, at least for the first half of the 20th century.

Seeing this burning cross was frightening. Fortunately, I only saw one as a child, but the KKK had a very real presence in our community, and this experience remains etched in my memory to this day.

The Ku Klux Klan had lain dormant for decades, but there was a revival with the release of D.W. Griffith's 1915 film, *The Birth of a Nation*, an adaptation of a play called the *Clansman* written by Thomas Dixon. This film was one of the most successful silent films ever made, grossing $10 million in its first run. The release was just 50 years after the Civil War, lasted three hours and recounts the beginning of slavery, the Civil War, the Freedman Bureau politics, the assassination of Lincoln, Reconstruction, and the eventual rise of the Ku Klux Klan. This historical melodrama is filled with racial tensions and some violence.

An Atlanta salesman and failed minister named William J. Simmons used the nostalgic 50th anniversary as an occasion to assemble a group of confederate sympathizers to revive the old Klan. It did not enjoy a great resurgence, and it took professional marketers Edward Clarke and Elizabeth Tyler to re-kindle the old Klan. A variety of economic, political and moral ailments lead to its eventual resurgence. In David Cunningham's book, *Klansville, U.S.A*, he gives a detailed account of the Klan's history. By 1925, there were between three and five million Klansmen in the USA—surprisingly, many of the strongest groups were in Ohio, Indiana, Oregon and Texas. Protestant morality and fraternal solidarity were the central themes and attracted both white and blue collar workers. Cunningham's book is a good source about the Klan's rise and fall and gives a particularly interesting account of its growth in North Carolina.

Many people posted subtle stickers on their windows to show their solidarity, i.e. *Keep Kool Kid* and *TWAK* meant *Trade With A Klansman*. There were also Women of the KKK and Junior Klan as ancillary appendage organizations of the KKK.

As a youngster, I remember hearing speculation about who was in the KKK because of the white sheets and secrecy associated with the group. People were also intimidated and maybe afraid this vigilante group might turn on them when least expected. By the latter part of the '60s, the KKK seemed to be shrinking, at least in Georgia. According to Cunningham, this was not the case in North Carolina, where it continued to flourish.

What my mother was to Laurie, Ellie Mae was to me—a second mother. Ellie Mae looked like Aunt Jemima, and she had the kindly disposition you would have expected from her smiling face on the advertisements. Ellie Mae probably was my first psychologist since I talked to her about everything. She knew everything there was to know about us anyway, so there were no secrets to hide. I would recount some of the things I had overheard and was puzzled about what they meant.

> "Lawdy mercy, Miss Joan, you got a memory like an elephant!" Ellie Mae would exclaim.

I could pour out all the hurt and anger I might have, and expect a sympathetic ear. She would never talk about my family but gave me many appropriate responses.

> "I just don't know why Miss Beatrice does some the things she does," she often remarked. Other replies might also be,
>
> "Lawdy mercy, Miss Joan, I just don't know how you remember so much!" Or, "You know your Daddy is a handsome man. I don't know why Ms Beatrice don't treat him better."

Rodney, Ellie Mae's husband, was a good natured, attractive black man; and when I was little, he used to carry me around on his shoulders. As I grew up, there wasn't any work he was doing that I was not privy to see. In the spring the piglets were castrated, and I used to help him hold the piglets down while he used a sharp razor to cut out the testicles. Then he would smear the cold tar on the wounds so they wouldn't become infected. He made repairs to the fences and took care of the few other animals we kept on the farm. We always had a steer that we were fattening for slaughter in the fall, about the time of hog killing. He let me help when the ducks were plucked for their down and soft feathers for comforters, feather beds, and pillows. Rodney could do almost anything. My family used to tell about one of the questions that I asked Rodney that became a laugh provoking family joke.

> I asked him, "Rodney if that is the mama cow, where is the papa cow?"
>
> "Good, Gawd, Miss Joan, I don't know!"

Periodically, Rodney also gathered the resin from the pine trees. The larger trees were cut through the bark so that a rectangular metal cup about ten inches long would fit under this gash and the tree would produce a thick, sticky substance, which was later converted into turpentine at a distillery. It was messy work and he had another man who helped him gather this cash crop. Because of the manual labor involved in this enterprise, it was one of the first things that fell by the wayside with the changing times.

If chicken was on the menu for dinner, someone had to kill the chicken. Just about any of the older people on the farm, including my grandmother knew how to wring a chicken's neck, but most of the time this task fell to Ellie Mae or to Otis Underhill, a second cousin of my grandmother. Scalding hot water was poured over the dead bird and it was systematically de-feathered by the plucking process. The smell was awful but the taste of the freshly fried chicken made the process a distant memory. Ellie Mae and my grandmother made the best fried chicken in the State of Georgia!

There were not many retirement pensions in those days and it was expensive to live alone, not to mention, the fear of living alone on a farm. There were always reports of escaped convicts roaming the countryside. Even in the 21st century, robberies and murders are still something people think about in the country as well as the city. Having Otis, my grandmother's cousin, live with us provided a measure of comfort for him and us; he became not only a security factor, but also a vital part of our lives.

He helped maintain the farm, along with Rodney. Otis was about five years older than my grandmother and it seemed they were always at cross-purposes. He took his orders from my grandmother, or Mama Parker, as we called her. She was his taskmaster! Mother understood him better, knowing he appreciated being asked rather than being told to do something. Consequently, they were great buddies. He was a grandfather figure to me. If I was about to get a spanking, he always came to my rescue.

Otis lived with us because he had never married and may have had a personality disorder. He could be cantankerous. The arrangement was, however, mutually beneficial for all concerned. I recall hearing his folks say he was crazy; but the truth of the matter was simple: he was a stubborn old goat! He may have had arrested tuberculosis, because my grandmother always washed his dishes with scalding hot water. He often scavenged the country store, which my family ran, for left over soft drinks in glass bottles. Otis loved Coca Cola and orange or grape Nehi.

He lived with us for over ten years, filling a void on the farm, which otherwise, would have been empty; it also kept Mama Parker from being lonely. His quarters were the extra bedroom built adjacent to the back porch. Once a week he bathed in our bathroom, but he used an outhouse, close to the chicken coop as a toilet. There was a sink and running water on the back porch, near his room where he shaved. Otis also made it possible for my mother and me to leave the farm and move to Savannah for five years. We came home on weekends to help out on the farm, but this period in the city might not have been possible if he had not been there for our entire family.

Otis's brother, Rayburn, lived in Miami, Florida, and always visited us at least once a year. Rayburn was a trained craftsman, and a man of means, with his own business. I can't remember if he was a carpenter or a mason; but he wore a Masonic ring with small diamonds. Otis was always impressed with the money his brother dropped in the church offering on Sunday when they went to the Baptist church. He enjoyed telling us what amount Rayburn had put in the collection plate. Otis was also one of the few people in my family, who did not seem conflicted about different religions. He attended the Baptist church mostly, but occasionally went to the Mormon Church as well. Otis read his Bible and reference books to better understand various passages.

I loved the mangoes that Rayburn brought us to eat. It was the most delicious fruit I had ever tasted. Some of the fruit grew in his backyard. Sometimes he spent the night, but often he traveled farther north to visit other relatives in Wilkinson County, where some of my grandmother's family had formerly lived.

Otis was such an essential part of our lives on the farm. What a difficult lesson it is to learn—none of us are indispensable. He died in January 14, 1957. I found an entry in my childhood diary:

> Otis died. Mama Parker helped him to the bathroom at 2:45AM and heard him cough around 4:00 AM. Ellie Mae came a few hours later to feed him breakfast but found him dead. I loved Otis.

This was my first experience with death and dying. It was my first funeral.

Ellie Mae had met many of my college friends over the years and was almost always supportive and gracious to all my friends. When I was a junior in college I brought my first serious boyfriend home. Harry was a Jewish guy from Boston. She was impressed with him and more hospitable than the rest of my family. My mother had actually met him on a visit to the University of GA and had been friendly with him. I had met him in a pre-med zoology class, he was my instructor.

He was a tall guy of Russian ancestry with dark hair and eyes. We dated for over a year; he was getting his PhD in marine biology and was a teaching instructor in 1963, between my junior and senior years at the University. I told him I was a Mormon and he laughed and said, "Usually, I am the one making such a statement, you know I am Jewish!" His family was always sending him delicious baked goods from Massachusetts, and he made sure to share them with me. The baked goods were part of his Jewish tradition. Harry was the first man who ever told me, "Joanie, you are a jewel." The warm feeling that compliment gave me has remained with me to this day.

We had a lot of fun. He was politically active and I went to lectures and discussions on topics that introduced me to new spheres of interest. When Harry came to visit at my home, my mother had a sick headache and could not talk with him; she spent most of the day in bed.

I don't remember many details about his visit, except he said, "I think your mom needs some help."

My home environment was certainly not friendly, but he persevered and remained in my life until my first year of medical school in 1964. I also took my other friends and him to visit my Uncle Earl and Aunt Bertha's home because they were more hospitable. I was never ashamed of my family, but they were unable to find interest in my friends, not only my male friends, but also my female friends.

One summer, while working in Utah, I met a girl from England. At the end of the season, Daphne and her friend, Nancy, bought an old car and decided to "See the USA." They stopped by my medical school to visit and later I invited them to the farm. Everyone was cold and unfriendly, and my mother talked only about her frizzy hair. It is a wonder my family was not sued, because our German Shepard bit her friend, Nancy, on the buttocks. It was so embarrassing. One night proved enough for my friends and they traveled on the next day, happy to escape.

It was fruitless to argue with my family. They had a way of making me feel bad and somehow they wound up being the victim. Mom and dad had many reasons for their actions, such as,

"We are looking out for you."

"You show bad judgment in picking friends."

"We have your best interest at heart."

"You are too good for him or her!"

My family formed snap judgments and didn't trust me to make my own decisions.

Anyway, later I received a farewell letter from Harry telling me he cared about me, but he feared for his life. Actually, my parents had called him, telling him that they had too much invested in my education and he should leave me alone, threatening him with bodily harm. It was shocking how little my personal views mattered to my parents and what a commodity I had become in their eyes. My well being counted for nothing as long as I performed as an outstanding student.

As an instructor Harry often wrote interesting quotes on the blackboard from the Persian philosopher, Omar Khayyam. One of his favorites was: *The moving finger writes, and having written moves on. Nor all thy piety nor thy wit, can cancel half a line of it.* Our relationship had been damaged beyond repair by my parents' action.

I loved Harry but not enough to marry him. It seemed as if there were too many obstacles in our path for a long-lasting relationship. He talked about moving to Boston and applying to medical school there. Having already been accepted at the state medical school, this did not appeal to me. As one of three women in the class, it didn't seem worth the effort to start over, having never traveled much farther north than Virginia. A short trip to New York City in 1962 with my dad for three days had not given me the best picture of the Northeast. There seemed too many uncertainties, to become rebellious and move to the North. I should have been outraged over my family telling him that I was a financial investment. My goal was to get the M.D. degree by continuing my studies, and hoping for better days to come. Maybe as a doctor, I would be better able to understand my family and myself.

In Harry's last letter to me, he once more quoted Khayyam, *There was a door to which I found no key: There was the veil through which I might not see.* He was very sad and so was I. We regretted what might have been.

We are not disturbed by things, but what we think about things.

> Epictetus, philosopher and
> advisor to Marcus Aurelius

Chapter Two
Savannah

My third grade teacher once made this remark on my report card, "Joan tends to daydream a lot." I probably had a lot on my mind, causing a confusion of emotions that small children find hard to express about their insecurities.

We resided on the farm with my grandmother, Laurie Holsworth Parker, who otherwise would have lived alone. In the early 1920's a divorced woman was not well accepted, it was a bit shameful, and she lived most of her life with little male companionship. I was her only granddaughter; there was definitely some competition over affection and discipline between her and my mother during my upbringing.

My grandmother was a tall woman who got a permanent wave two to three times a year; she wore her hair short and curled with a side part. She had a good sense of humor and a twinkle in her eye. Although she had thin legs and walked slightly pigeon-toed, she was nevertheless, a slim attractive woman who always looked neat in her cotton dresses and aprons. I hardly ever saw her without her apron at home. She also wore a bonnet or straw hat when she went out in the sunshine. The hot, Georgia, sun made skin thick, blotchy and leathery, so she did the best she could without the benefit of sunscreen lotion.

I sensed a conflict between my mother and grandmother, but it was hard to put into words. I loved them both, but often respected my grandmother more than Mother. I felt secure with grandmother and called her "Mama" the same as my mother did. She loved me a great deal. It was from her that I got my sex education, as twisted and distorted as it was; however, she meant well. She was predictable and reliable, two very important qualities for child rearing. My mother related more than once that I told her, "Mother, sometimes I feel like YOUR MOTHER."

Mama Parker had two children, Beatrice, my mother, and a son Earl. Learning as a child that her husband, Willis, had left her, was an eye-opener. Because she had refused to go to Kentucky with him to live, their marriage was dissolved after seven years of separation. His own family farmed there, and they were pulling him homeward. Grandmother had visited her husband by train several times in Kentucky, but she never could bring herself to leave her own family in Georgia. No one knows, in addition to their own interpersonal family problems, there may have been some remaining regional prejudices. [I found out recently that Kentucky did not send many soldiers to fight with the Confederacy during the Civil War.] In addition, my grandparents lived in the early part of the 20th century, when travel and communication were not easy. I grew up knowing him as Grandpa Parker and his second wife was referred to as Zina. The Willis Parkers did not become real to me until the late 1940's.

I am not quite sure what brought Grandpa Parker back to Georgia for a visit in 1948, since it had been almost three decades. It may just have been the second wife's curiosity to see the first wife. A strange reunion it must have been, but don't recall many details. Mother was 35 years old and Uncle Earl was 31, and I was four. He came with Zina and their three boys; the youngest must have been about 14. Earl surely wanted to know his father better and Grandpa Parker was looking for closer ties to his oldest son, who was born in 1917. All of this bonding must have been difficult for my mother, since she was very protective of her younger brother, even though he was over 30 years old. Growing up on the farm, they were like two peas in a pod.

Grandpa Parker and his family visited at my Uncle Earl's home which was about 100 miles east, and after a few days everyone drove up to the farm for a family gathering.

The high point of their stay was hearing my Aunt Bertha exclaim, "I'm not staying in the same house with a man and his two wives!"

Uncle Earl responded in a soft voice, "Now, Bertha, calm down, it will be alright."

Of course, everyone knew the Mormons had been polygamists and I guess she had visions of his hopping from one bed to the other. My Aunt Bertha had been reared as a strict Jehovah's Witness, and looking back, I can see how she thought it was strange. It certainly was inappropriate by many standards. In reality, the reunion of her husband's divorced parents after such a long time was mind-boggling. Bertha had a hard time adjusting to these somewhat unusual circumstances. The older I have gotten, the more I appreciate my aunt's impulsive remarks. Uncle Earl calmed her down and apparently there weren't any more rifts. Everyone went to bed, but there probably wasn't much sleep.

Aunt Bertha told me after I was married, when I was 26 years old, she thought Grandpa Parker's reappearance into their lives had been the beginning of Mother's self-destructive tendencies. She also informed me, against Uncle Earl's wishes, that Mama Parker had been pregnant when Grandpa married her. The child she was carrying, my mother, was not his, so my mother was in essence illegitimate. I do

At the Crossroads: A Southern Daughter's Story

not know if she was raped or what happened; an elderly cousin told me years later that my grandmother became pregnant from a Mormon missionary, but it was not Willis Parker. However, the knot had been tied, and no one knows what was said after he found out. The marriage lasted five years, on paper at any rate, and Earl was born from the union. He was less than a year old and Mom was five when Grandpa Parker left. His reappearance in our families' lives must have been staggering, showing up as he did with a new wife and three grown sons.

Once the relationships had been re-established, Zina became an avid correspondent and I'm sure she had been exchanging letters with Earl before my family came into the picture. Earl's only son, Willis, was named after his grandfather. There was a great interest on the part of my mother to find out what and when they had heard from Zina. On occasions my mother, Beatrice, would snoop around their house, given the chance, looking for any news—a sibling's jealousy and a longing for wholeness that seemed to elude her.

Zina was an energetic woman with a nervous smile. She was 10 years younger than her husband Willis. After I finished my graduate studies and was living in Utah for a year in the late 1960's, she made a spontaneous confession to me.

> "I only had sex with Willis three times and each time I became pregnant! Her words implied that he did not enjoy sex. I just sat there with a poker face and exclaimed, "Zina that is truly amazing, unbelievable!"

I did not understand this confession and in later years pondered why she told me this intimate story. Later I realized in many religions, divorce and remarriage, though acceptable in the eyes of the law, in the "eye of God" it is considered adulterous. Perhaps she thought this confession made her seem less flawed. I am neither a biblical or religious scholar, but she had decided I would be her Confessor.

But there was another side to Zina. She had grown up in Colorado. She knew a lot about nutrition—she always extolled the benefits of potassium and her knowledge served her well because she lived an active life until she was 100 years old. She was of German descent, amiable and talkative. On the other hand, Grandpa was pleasant enough, but by no means loquacious; he could have even been described as stoic in nature. By the time I got to know them better, he was in his 70's and seemed to be slowing down quite a bit due to adult onset diabetes and high blood pressure.

Like some Mormons that I have known, they were interested in money and some times bragged a little. Real estate was how some of the family made their money—fixing up property then flipping it. I had never been exposed to boastful people; my mother may have bragged occasionally, but my father was suspicious of such people. He would rather play dumb and poor than appear to be more than he was.

The Western folk had a keen interest in what we had and what my dad was doing to earn money. The fact that my dad had his own business was a novelty for the family. They had either been farm boys or worked for someone else. Seeing my dad's pecan operation probably was inspiring to them. Later, the youngest of the sons established a nursery and landscaping business, doing quite well. The older brothers stayed on as drivers with the Greyhound Bus, and also did some property speculation. They all were handsome men especially the younger two; they were over 6 feet tall, blond, and blue eyed and had an athletic body build.

During my medical internship in Utah, Zina complained that Willis was hard on their children when they were small.

They had a dairy farm in the early years of their marriage and cows require a lot of heavy work. The farmer who takes care of his animals has to be a tough taskmaster. The three boys escaped as soon as they could. The youngest, Elwin, went to the University of Utah and got a good education after serving in the Air Force like his brother. He was most likely the first in his family to graduate from college.

Thirty years is a long time and it is hard to build relationships with people after such a long separation even if there were letters over the years. Mother must have known Willis wasn't her dad. One could see she was jealous of the bond he tried to cultivate with her brother. She often said to him "He's not your dad. He's never been a father to us."

No matter how well guarded a secret may be, children have a way of sensing things. Mama Parker never talked badly about her former husband, it was just the opposite; she always said he was a good man. The stories mother told me about him painted him as a strict, unaffectionate man. As I came to know him years later, I think this was a fair assessment. He was an impressive man as far as size, he must have been 6' 3"and his second wife, Zina, was no more than 5'tall. Some people say big men like little women and this was certainly true in their case. His gene was the dominant one for the height of their children—all stood six feet or taller.

My mother told me how Grandpa would prompt her to tell what people called her: "Aunt Helen calls me Honeybunch, Grandma calls me Butterfly, but Grandpa calls me Puss." It made a funny joke for a four-year-old to relate, but she suspected the joke was on her, because everyone always enjoyed a good laugh.

Mother and I were living in Savannah the next time the Parkers came for a visit, I must have been around nine years old. They did not go to the farm this time, instead visited the small town, where my Aunt Bertha and Uncle Earl lived. It was about an hour's drive from Savannah. Eventually, their visit led to further alienation for my mother, although there was not any conflict that I recall. She began to feel more and more like an outsider, but she did try to bridge the gap.

She offered our apartment to Uncle Earl when they came to Savannah. Uncle Earl's son Willis wore braces on his teeth, so they made frequent trips to see the orthodontist who was located a few blocks from our apartment on Jones Street. It was a great place for them to hang out for the day or as an overnight accommodation. My mom and I were generally at the farm on weekends when the appointments were scheduled, so there was very little social interaction. Once I remember leaving some soiled panties in the bathroom sink to soak. Mother had not told me that they would be coming, so I was suitably mortified that they had seen them.

My Aunt Bertha's perceptions about Mother's deterioration were accurate. After the first visit in 1948, my mother started having some rough times, especially in her marriage. My dad was not a Mormon; he had been brought up Baptist and did not have a lot of interest in religion.

I didn't ask a lot of questions, yet had a feeling that my parents weren't madly in love. Often I wondered what kept them together. Mother was trying to live down the fact that she had been caught driving drunk a couple of times. I was with her more than once when she had an accident, and those times scared the daylights out of me. One time as we were driving on a country dirt road, she ran into a tree. We weren't badly injured, but she got a cut over her eye, and I thought for sure she was going to bleed to death.

Before the age of eight, I had been in three car wrecks with her. Once the car was parked on a precarious embankment and had we rolled over we would have been severely maimed or killed. Luckily the police came upon us. To be cited for DUI (Driving under the Influence) for a woman in a small rural county at that time, was like wearing a scarlet letter on your sleeve. Drinking crippled her in so many ways, especially when she found out one of my classmates referred to her as a "Drunk." This embarrassment prompted her to bring Valentine's Day cookies for my whole class. She wasn't happy until years later, when she had someone expunge it from the record in the county court house. She was politically connected and was always involved in local elections.

Mother was also getting over another, even more traumatic episode in her life. She was not happy with her lot in life and often talked nostalgically about her former boyfriends. There had been a fellow named Bob whom she met at college and a priest she met while in nursing school, who she claimed wanted to give up his vocation to marry her.

These stories were like fairy tales to me and sometimes I'd ask, "Well, Mother, how come you didn't marry Bob?" She said, Grandpa said, "Well, I will 'Bob' him if he shows his face around here. Besides I was ashamed my house wasn't good enough."

Many years later after my mom's death, I came across a love letter she had received from an old flame by the name of Harold, a former missionary in Georgia. He must have been very infatuated with her. His letter was addressed to her on Lancaster Ave, Tampa, Florida, where she was on a church mission

It was dated June 22, 1937. It was written from California.

> *"Good evening, Darling,*
>
> *Boy, oh, boy is it a grand evening here. Such a large and beautiful moon is out and it is so warm and cozy. The folks were having company and so I grabbed my tablet and came on up to the park to write to you. There is from one to three couples under each tree whispering sweet nothings in each others ears, and here I am all alone, but only in*

body. My thoughts are entirely of you. So kid, I heard today that if a person is out of work down there (Georgia) they will put you on the chain gang and if a person comes into Georgia looking for work, they have to get work within three weeks. How true is it? What kind of work is there to be hjad down there?

I really and truly expected a letter from you today but never got any. It sort of turned the day into a dreary one for me. Tonight we had three auto lubrications which wasn't [sic] bad for a fellow like me. I am trying my best to find something that pays more money so that I can get enough ahead to carry me thru for a little while down South. Bea, what would you suggest would be the best thing to do? I would appreciate any advice you can offer. What are your plans? Yesterday, since it was my day off, I started out to that Borax mine, but found out it was three hundred miles to it. If you have a map you can find Pasadena and then run your pencil along the line going East thru Arcadia, Monrovia, Azusa, Glendora and Claremont on to San Bernardino, then turn North on US 66 to US 395 then on to 466 to Kramer and the mine is just two miles out from the town. It gets awfully hot in the summer, but you can get $5 per day for 8 hours of work. If I could earn $175, I would have a good start to come see you."

[Then he dropped the bombshell on her, He had a wife and kid!]

"Do you think I am doing something wrong in not living with someone I don't care for after there is a baby in the family? He surely is a cute little tyke

> *and he surely takes to me. He calls me Daddy. Oh, Beatrice, why do things happen like that? If I come down South it means giving him up. I love you and him but you are not his mother. Gee, it sure is a terrible mix up. But, Darling, time can heal that.*
>
> *Gee, I would lose almost everything if I gave up Leo and Gloria and then I couldn't even win you. No mail again this morning. I really am getting frantic. Honey, can't you send me at least two letters a week? Bea, why do you have to be so far away; it takes ages and ages for a letter to get here from you. Can't you give me a little encouragement?"*

[The letter went on for three more pages and finally closed with]

> *Darling, send me the phone number of the place you are staying and I'll call you some time. Yours as ever and for always, with loads of love, Harold"*

My mother and father were married in the fall of 1937, so I'm sure this had something to do with her not writing back, and it would have been hard to encourage a man to leave an unwed mother and a little boy. She must have been heartbroken and probably thought of her own early childhood. I really don't know how long my parents had known one another. Raymond Johnson, or Ray as he was sometimes called, probably had sold some vegetables or fruit to my great grandfather's country store. He had a regular route and was more of a peddler in those days. He bought and sold anything on which he could make some money. Ray was handsome and could be charming in a self deprecating way that country folks like. Later he established his shelled pecan business and did quite well. Dad was an affable, hard-working man.

My mom and dad stuck together even though their road was rocky at times. I sensed Mother's unhappiness for a long time, but the seriousness of it showed itself when she took me along to see a boyfriend. Even though I was only five or six years old at the time, whatever remnants of loyalty there was to my father, were incited in me. As a small child, I instinctively knew what she was doing wasn't right. Still, in spite of these ambivalent feelings, I remained loyal to her. Without even saying anything to anyone about this episode, my dad found out about it and he gave my mother a real beating. She had two black eyes in a swollen face and she didn't go out for weeks.

The beating was extremely frightening for me to witness. Mother and Mama Parker were sleeping together and Dad grabbed her out of bed like a madman obsessed by the devil. Bang! Slap! Yell! Of course, I was trembling like crazy, thinking my mom would surely be killed. He brought in an axe and chopped out the telephone. It was an old-fashioned wall phone, and when he ripped it out, it left a terrible hole that served as a reminder of our family's traumatic night. Yelling and screaming, I picked up a piece of wood from the wood box by the space heater and wanted to hit him with it.

I was crying out, "No, Daddy, don't hit Mother any more." My protective instinct came to the fore.

Decades later I wondered if this did not do some damage to her brain. She at least had a bad concussion and some damage to the frontal lobes. Her whole face was swollen, especially around the eyes. The skin turned black and blue and then hues of yellow and green as the blood was absorbed. The healing took weeks and was a frightening reminder for me to see as a small child. Wife beating for adultery was an accepted form of punishment for a woman, and her mother's reaction added to Mother's misery.

At the Crossroads: A Southern Daughter's Story

My grandmother was screaming, but she only encouraged him. "Let her have it, Ray, she's been running around on you." What a madhouse it was that night. No wonder my mother had ambivalent feelings about her mother. She was twice scorned, once by Ray and then her own mother.

Her brother Earl came soon after the beating, but I was so small that I don't remember any details. Mother really had no defenders. She wore the Scarlet Letter of an adulterous woman now. Only with time would she be able to live it down.

Later as a doctor, I read more about frontal lobe injury. Harm to this area of the brain has an impact on divergent thinking, flexibility, impulse control and problem solving. One of the most common effects of frontal lobe damage can be a dramatic change in social behavior. This may have been the case with my mother.

After Mother recovered, she never let my father or grandmother forget what they had said and done. No mention was ever again made of her affair—at least not in my presence—but my dad, Ray and Mama Parker carried remorse the rest of their lives. They were sorry for what had occurred that night. She let them know she was a victim. Over the next couple of years, she pulled herself together and separated from my dad. We still came back to the farm on week ends, but we were in Savannah during the week.

The move to Savannah was one of the happiest periods of my life. Beatrice got a new lease on life by getting away from the farm, her mother and my dad. Self-image and self worth are so important to our well-being. I agree with my aunt, that the Parkers re-entering our life, may have contributed to my mother's disintegration and reinforced her inferiority complex. She was in her thirties by then, but it takes a long time for an adult to see their parents as people with all their weaknesses and flaws and not lay blame on the human condition. This illegitimacy lay at the root of her feeling alone—as a psychiatrist friend of mine said, "Always an orphan, always looking for wholeness."

My parents' marriage had hit the skids some years before the move to Savannah. Mother was suffering from depression because of the affair she had or because of the beating she had taken from my dad when he found out about it. Eventually the hurt manifest itself as aggression toward my dad. She purchased a hand gun and my dad got a Gulf Stream trailer, parking it in the yard.

One day I heard pop, pop, pop followed by, "If you ever lay a hand on me again, you SOB, I'll kill you." He quickly dodged the bullets and headed for his Gulf Stream trailer. I knew they had both done wrong, so it was difficult for a child to figure this all out. I had skipped a grade in school and was making an adjustment to the third grade; hence, daydreaming was part of my school day. My head was filled with so many traumatic events from home; it was sometimes overwhelming and difficult to concentrate.

It wasn't long after these incidents that my father took me on our first trip together. He had purchased his dream car, a second hand Studebaker coupe, and we headed for the western coast of Florida for a few days. I remember overhearing my grandfather talking to my dad saying, "That child is growing up and she doesn't even know who you are!"

He took this admonition from his dad to heart and we spent a wonderful few days together. It was easy to fall in love with Gulfport, Mississippi and the whole area of Panama City Beach with their beautiful white sand and bluish green waters. My first Ferris wheel ride was with my dad and we never laughed so much or so hard. We saw people dance on the beach, and he loved to tell the story about my saying, "Daddy, you better watch out, I'm going to tell mother, you have been looking at those girls dancing "the cat."

At the Crossroads: A Southern Daughter's Story

My mom enjoyed her job in Savannah as a grade school teacher. The Robbeys, from whom we rented a two-bedroom apartment, were super people. We lived in their third floor apartment. Jones Street was part of the historic district of Savannah; it was a cobbled stoned street with live oak, poplar trees, and many azaleas as well as camellia bushes. All of Savannah with its many parks and squares, was spectacular in the spring, especially our neighborhood, where we lived for five years. The Robbeys often took me to concerts and invited me to practice my music on their piano. Mrs. Robbey was always baking, creating mouthwatering, delicious cakes. The smells wafted out of their apartment on the first floor and filled the stairway to our apartment.

Jones Street was only a few blocks from my mom's school on Barnard Street. I entered the fifth grade at the same school, but I remember she was not at all impressed with my teacher. Especially after my telling her, Mrs. Cooper had us copying the social studies book, instead of teaching.

Beatrice proved herself to be a good teacher. She gained back some of her self respect, and was even shown as a model teacher by a local TV station, performing with her rhythm band of third grade students. Children loved her and she had a real talent for listening and communicating with them. As a teacher she had brought several children home with her even when we lived on the farm. They were often "orphan" children who perhaps had a family but no one to take time with them. I didn't totally understand having these children occasionally in our home and was really a bit jealous.

Being on television was quite something in those days. After the program aired, a write up in the Savannah Newspaper highlighted another event at the school;

> "The Mexican Hat Dance was performed by Mrs. Johnson's third graders. During the May Day festival at Barnard Street School Mrs. Raymond

Johnson's booth was decorated with a painting of a Mexican festival, with balloons, roses and straw hats. The festival was well attended by the local community."

This was my first exposure to life in a big city, and I was given cautionary warnings about not talking to strangers, never taking any candy, and always walking as though I had a destination. Since my mother had to stay longer at the school, I was a latch key kid. However, my grandmother some times came to Savannah and stayed with us for the week, especially if it was a short week like Thanksgiving, Christmas, or Easter. She would dutifully watch me cross busy Drayton Street, giving her the OK sign, as she looked out from the third floor window. My dad came occasionally to visit, often spending the night. He was trying to make a go of his marriage; this made me happy when they were together. Many times he would visit his oldest brother, Uncle Carl, who lived in Savannah and combined the trip with a visit with us. We really didn't have any fun outings as a family.

Savannah offered many wonderful opportunities available for me; perhaps, these opportunities were not appreciated at the time. At the Conservatory of Music, I had music lessons, even though we did not have a piano in the city. I had taken music lessons before and we had a piano at the farm, where we were every weekend. Practicing occasionally at our landlords, the Robbeys, was a bit awkward. In addition to the music lessons, there were tap and ballet lessons, not to mention my favorite-evenings at the movies. Being an attractive little girl with gumption, the studio asked me, during my second year, to perform with another student, on a local TV show called, "Happy Dan, the Story Man." All my mother's friends and relatives tuned in to watch the show and I felt pretty special in a festive costume. Missing a step or two, it plagued me afterwards, but my audience reassured me they had not noticed!

We loved the movies, especially the double feature evenings. Walking everywhere in Savannah, my mom and I became really good buddies. It was a chance for my mother to have me all to herself away from Mama Parker, who could be a critical person at times. Who knows what molds our character. I loved my grandmother very much and did not see this conflict between the two, mother and daughter, until much reflection in later years. These years with my mother were some of the happiest of our lives.

After my year at Barnard Street School, the principal recommended a parochial school to my mother. For the next three years, I attended Cathedral of St. Johns Day School run by the Sisters of Mercy, not only learning good study habits, but also becoming more obsessively compulsive about certain things. My shoes were placed in a certain way, habits such as not stepping on a crack while walking to school and other rituals that became habits. Thankfully I no longer recollect them all! Additionally, Sister Agnes put a stop to the nonsense of putting little circles above the small letter "I"! As a doctor, I now realize this was my way of controlling my world, which had been up to this point, so topsy-turvy, filled with stress.

I was a good student with a gift for memorizing poems, and could even recite the Declaration of Independence by heart. In the ninth grade, I entered St Vincent's Academy studying there for a year until we moved back to the farm and gave up the apartment. It was good to be home with my grandmother, but it was about this time that my mother decided to go back to the Georgia Teachers College to finish her degree in Education. Beatrice had been going to summer school to earn credits toward her Baccalaureate degree in teaching for a long time. Even though the college was a long way from the farm, it was now or never for her to reach this milestone. About two quarters of further study were needed for her to finish all her requirements for graduation.

Mother enrolled me in the College's Lab School for children of college students. It was a good school, but it meant leaving early in the morning and returning late in the day by car. Being so sleepy, resting my head on my mother's lap, I looked forward to another hour of sleep before starting the school day. Honestly, I don't know how we did it, but this went on for the better part of the school year. The times were changing, so no advancement could be made as a teacher without a Bachelor of Science degree. When she walked down the aisle with her diploma in 1958, we were all proud of her. For some reason, my father was not at her graduation, but Mama Parker, as well as my Uncle Earl and Aunt Bertha, were there.

Whenever my mother was taking classes in the summer, my grandmother was my principal caregiver. Mother probably had a room at the college, because I looked forward to Fridays when she returned home. She almost always surprised me with some popular sheet music that would draw me to the piano for practice or brought a mystery book for me to read late into the night.

On one occasion when my mom was traveling back and forth to college to get her B.S. degree, a most peculiar event occurred. She suffered a bout of what I recognize now as hysteria. She lost her voice and couldn't speak. She had had hyperthyroidism when she was in her late teens and at first the doctor thought it might be related to this. After seeing several doctors, finally one said to her,

> "Go back to where you lost your voice and you will find it again". Powerful words! She did just that and she started speaking again.

On other occasions, she would move her lips as if she was talking to someone. I now recognize this episode as schizoid behavior. It was most disturbing to watch if you were in the car with her.

> Sometimes asking, "Mother, who are you talking to?" She would respond, "Oh, no one, I was just remembering a conversation."

My father was more or less a background figure until I was 13 or 14 years old. He was running his shelled pecan business and managing fairly well, but it meant long hours on the road. He traveled as far as Bristol, Virginia, and as far south as Miami in the early days. Since his truck was empty on the return trips home, he often picked up discarded items from the richer neighborhoods. For a while we had a number of overstuffed chairs. He had grown up poor, and saw added value remaining in the furniture planted on the sidewalk.

If my mother needed extra money, she just stole some of my father's pecans from a storage trailer parked at the farm. He probably didn't keep a careful inventory and she was like a mouse nibbling away from a big pile of pecans. However, she made me a partner in her crimes. It was my job to squeeze through a small window at the front of the tandem trailer and hand her five to seven pounds until the 100-pound sack was empty. Naturally, it took me quite sometime to accomplish this task. I didn't have to play cops and robbers; the reality was better than fantasy. She would sell the pecans in Savannah to another dealer. She constantly complained that Ray was too stingy.

While we lived in Savannah I really enjoyed the times Mama Parker came to stay with us in the city. It was nice having her at home after school. It also was fun for me to be on the farm with my grandmother, so on a few occasions, when I was older and had more of a school break, my mom would put me on the bus and someone would pick me up at the bus station, which was about 40 minutes from the farm.

As a ten year old, and a latch key kid, it was my job to light the gas oven and cook the frozen Swanson chicken potpies. The pies were delicious and my favorite. Initially, I was afraid the house was going to blow to pieces when the oven was lit. Because there was no pilot light, one had to be extra cautious. It was also my job to take the trash down the fire escape to the larger containers at the back of the house. I tried not to look down those open stairs and do this task as quickly as possible.

In the evenings, we mostly listened to the radio. Programs such as "The Jack Benny Show" and "Amos 'n' Andy" were the ones we heard; they were broadcasted out of Cincinnati, Ohio. We talked about buying a TV, but often went to the movies, which were in Technicolor by then; television was still black and white. We would think twice about going to a black and white movie—color was our preference. The double features were a special attraction. Love stories were my favorite kind of movie.

My love for the movies started early with my mother's cousin, Danny and his wife Vivian. They went to the movies every Saturday and would stop by the farm and ask permission from my parents to take me along. They had no children and loved to spoil me with fun games. Anyway, I also loved being with them, especially when they went to the movies. It was date night for them, dressed in their finest clothes with spotlessly polished shoes.

My trips to the movies with Vivian and Danny often postponed the occasional bowel cleanse at the farm. Calomel tablets or Castoria were used to accomplish this and both were awful. I hated this procedure and later learned the poisonous nature of the treatment; calomel is mercurous chloride, which was eventually removed from the market because of heavy metal poisoning. Castor oil was also a favorite, but our family mostly reserved it for bad colds.

I loved the Esther Williams movies and her swimming—I myself was afraid of the water and my grandmother reinforced this fear. Once though, because of my fondness for her movies, my mother took me to a rural swimming hole. When my grandmother saw me in the water, she ran into the water with her shoes and stockings yelling and screaming,

"Stop, you are going to drown that child!"

Beatrice did not know how to swim either, but she wanted me to learn. Years later, we learned together after many trips to a local public swimming pool. I also learned to trust her in the water when we had vacations in St Augustine, Florida. We would jump the waves together holding each other's hands.

Living in Savannah had been wonderful, but I had little time on the weekends to develop any kind of friendships among my classmates. We might have continued living in the city, had it not been for the death of Otis, my grandmother's cousin. He was my surrogate grandfather saving me from many a spanking. He was a simple man and often read his bible when he was resting. Losing him suddenly would change our lives in ways we could not imagine. Mama Parker was frequently alone now and did not like living in the rural area all by herself. We returned to the farm the summer before I started the 10th grade. My parents were also living together again. They had never formally separated.

I spent the next three years at a county school and developed closer ties with the rural kids from my community. Beatrice went out of her way to see that I got a good education and everyone at the new county school marveled at my discipline and good study habits. The kids in my class were all friendly, mostly farmers' kids, and it wasn't long before I found my niche. I was quite good at remembering people's names and by the 11th grade was chosen class president. Joining several school clubs, happy to be among some girls who were friendly; I felt a sense of community.

My mother taught school in an adjoining county; she would drop me off at school and drive about 20 minutes to her school where she taught fifth grade. She had begun her career with a two-year certificate, finally getting her Bachelor's in 1958. There was a real shortage of teachers in rural areas in 1934, when Mother began her career in the adult literacy program . She remarked how she used to walk many miles a day to get around to all the communities that were in her literacy program. She got to know a lot of people in the county and was quite respected in the community. Because she had been to nursing school for a year, she was often sought after to give a pain shot or other injections by the local doctor.

If my mother had been born in another time, she might have entered politics, because politics fascinated her. She was the type of person who used her political connections. When I applied to medical school, she secured a letter of recommendation from the Governor of Georgia, Carl Saunders. When I went for my interviews, the doctors interviewing me appeared to be more impressed by his letter than by my credentials. I was more than qualified to be admitted, but it never hurts to put icing on the cake. Beatrice was an early feminist and as a somewhat younger woman said to me years later, "She was a woman ahead of her time."

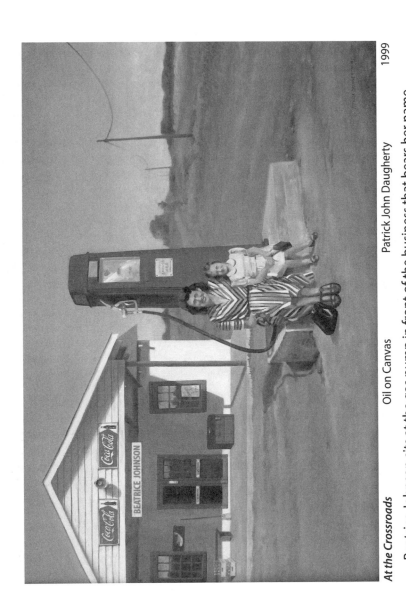

At the Crossroads Oil on Canvas Patrick John Daugherty 1999

Beatrice Johnson sits at the gas pump in front of the business that bears her name. Her young daughter Joan is smiling as they wait at the crossroads.

The superior man is intelligently, not blindly, faithful.

Confucius

Chapter Three
The Mormons

We were by no means a devout Mormon family, but it was a real presence in our lives. The visiting Mormon "Elders", as they are called, dropped by often and were invited for meals and sometimes overnight stays. I was baptized when I was nine, which is the recommended age for baptism in the Mormon faith. This was the age of accountability, and my sins were now my own. The Lord wouldn't blame my Mom or Dad any longer. My baptism took place in a creek outside Savannah soon after we moved there.

The Mormon religion is truly the first American religion, founded by Joseph Smith near Palmyra in the western part of the state of New York. Mormonism set itself apart as the only true religion of Jesus Christ. Smith restored it after receiving visions from the angel Moroni in the vicinity of his home at a place he later called Hill Cumorah. The story of how this happened is filled with mystery and hints of the occult. As Jon Krakauer says in his book, about the origins of Mormonism, *Under the Banner of Heaven:*

> There was an appealing simplicity to the Book of Mormon's central message, which framed existence as an unambiguous struggle between good and evil. There are two churches only; the one is the church of the Lamb of God, and the other is the church of the devil; whoso belongeth not to the church of the Lamb of God, belongeth to that great church, which is the mother of abominations.

My mom's religious values were learned in her early years of rural missionary exposure. The Mormon missionaries kept in touch with their members, keeping them involved. We attended church on Sunday evenings, going occasionally to prayer meetings. There was some socializing with a few Mormon friends, but we were often on the farm during the weekends, so we were not heavily involved in a lot of church activities. Church services were usually held in the mornings: families were encouraged to use Sunday evenings as family time. The evening church in Savannah was an exception.

The farm had been inherited by my grandmother from her father. It was where my mother had grown up. During my early childhood, there was nobody with whom I could share any kind of puzzlement about religion. My great grandpa Holsworth had been one of the first Latter Day Saints (Mormon) converts, and then the rest of the family eventually became members. The Mormons were probably more progressive and fun loving than any other churches found in rural communities; after all, they liked to dance. There was less fire and damnation in the sermons. Since my mother was a teacher, the emphasis on knowledge and learning set well with her. One of the favorite sayings in the Mormon Church was, "the glory of God is intelligence."

The "Elders" were usually from the West, were almost always young, good-looking men, who traveled in pairs and drove the American Motors' Ramblers; Mother said that George Romney, the president of the company, was a Mormon, so maybe the church got a good deal on the cars. Elder Brimley was my elder and I fantasized as a young girl that when I grew up we'd get married and live "happily ever after"—a young girl's crush. From him I learned the church history and why baptism was important. I recall thinking, I didn't really understand it all, but figured there was no point in arguing.

As a child, it seemed Joseph Smith's martyrdom and Jesus Christ's crucifixion had a lot in common. Smith seemed like a mighty brave fellow; he was a real pioneer and my love for the underdog, as he was portrayed, made it easy for me to identify with him. The story was gruesome. The Mormons first settled in Nauvoo, Illinois, but were later persecuted, forcing them to leave the state. Because they were displaced, they moved farther west looking for sanctuary. Crossing the Great Plains was no easy task.

"Why would people do a thing like that, Mother?" I asked. "Oh, honey, he was different and people were afraid of him, I guess." The history of Joseph Smith fascinated me well into my adulthood, but I later read some extremely unfavorable reports of his behavior, especially toward women; he was a polygamist extraordinaire. Jon Krakauer's book, *Under the Banner of Heaven*, was a page turning novel for a former Mormon and it helped to explain some of the events that had taken place in the Mormon Church, I had not understood as a child. There was a lot of violence in the early church history that Krakauer explained more clearly. After Smith's death, Brigham Young became their leader. When he got to the Utah territory, he uttered the now famous words,

"This is the Place!" Located in the mountains overlooking the Salt Lake Valley of Utah, most of the Mormons came to reside in Utah and the Western states.

The Mormons that I came to know through the church were all good people and their norms were the ones that later influenced me. Some Mormons had an explanation for everything, and according to them strict adherence to Mormonism could change anything. Being in the Mormon Church kept me focused and goal oriented. Through two strong religions, the Mormons and the Catholics, I learned discipline and good study habits. The four years in parochial school in Savannah proved invaluable. Sheer determination kept me going through all my studies, especially through college and later in medical school. Later, these qualities were the factors that earned me admission to the premed program at the University of Georgia. My dream became a reality when I obtained my M. D. degree at the age of 24.

There are many things in the world around us that needed to be changed, but the crusade of improvement was mostly directed toward my daddy and Grandpa Johnson, who were Baptists of the most fundamental type. "Hard-shelled Baptists," as they were called, were about as tough as hickory nuts; their theology was hard on anyone around them who was not a Baptist. They were as inflexible as the Mormons. There were times, however, when Mother had tried to embrace the Baptist Church. So I grew up in this Baptist/Mormon household, where I heard quite a bit of conflicting theology. It was really more a conflict of wills, as much as any kind of Christian principles. Later in life as I came to know other religions, I realized the Mormons were not as Christ centered.

One time Mother wanted very much to get involved with the local Baptist church. She had been befriended by the minister and started attending the Bible study with a friend. She must have enjoyed it a lot because she remarked over the years about how well the class went and how she was able to impart some of her knowledge of the Bible.

There was a change in ministers and I guess the next pastor was not as flexible. When he found out that Mother was a Mormon he told her, "You ought to be attending your own church." That brash remark caused a lot of hostility; none of us, including my father, ever forgot it. After all, the closest Mormon Church was thirty-five miles away.

If the elders stayed long enough and got to know us as a family, sooner or later they heard the story of how my Grandpa Parker had deserted my Grandma Parker (nee Holsworth) and her two little children. We had a guest room that was the best bedroom in the house and the elders were always invited to stay over if they wanted. Several did become good friends of the family. The more they chastised Grandpa Parker for being such a sinful man, the better friends they became, especially with my mother.

Of course, the part about Mama Parker's not wanting to leave home was always conveniently left out, and Grandpa Parker was made to sound like an irresponsible no good scoundrel by Mother. Mama Parker never said much, leaving a lot to speculation. Many years later, as an adult, when I had the opportunity to speak with Grandpa Parker and hear his side of the story, I understood why she was mostly silent. My grandmother was the eldest daughter, her mother was sickly, and her family was pulling on her heartstrings, according to him. He told me, he overheard them talking once. When her parents said, "You don't know what he will do to you when he gets you up there in Kentucky!"

He had his own regrets though, and he must have been a little weak and a bit of a coward. When he returned after an absence of almost three decades with his second wife and three boys, Mama Parker asked him for a few moments in private. He told me, "You know I never did take the time to find out what she wanted to tell me." It seemed to me, he never got over the guilt of his own lack of initiative.

Maybe he was afraid of his second wife. How sad that he had so little time or charity for my grandmother, whom he left with two children to rear. In all probability it would not have been an easy life with such a man. Even his second wife, Zina told me he was a hard man to live with.

Many of the arguments between Mother and Dad were over religions. Apparently, my dad, Ray, whom many people called by his last name of Johnson, had promised he would become a Mormon when he married Mother, but for one reason or another it never happened. The only time I went to church with my dad was at Christmas. We went to the Methodist Church in his hometown in an adjoining community; they usually read the Christmas story from the Bible and the children all dressed up as Joseph, Mary, the Baby Jesus and the Shepherds. After the singing, large one-inch thick candy canes were passed out to the congregation. It was most enjoyable being with my dad at Christmas, but Mom never went with us. She always had the excuse that she just didn't feel like it. I used to think if only Dad would become a Mormon, then we could all live happily ever after. He was not critical of Mormons; he just didn't want to be one.

Since my grandmother and my mother were Mormons, I'm sure the old Mormon tradition of storing a year's supply of food was initiated or, at the very least, reinforced our tendency to squirrel away food for hard times. My family could all remember the depression of the late 1920s and '30s, so when the food supply was plentiful, it was only prudent to store up for leaner times. The Mormon history itself was one of hardship—moving from Illinois to Missouri, then on to Utah. Growing up with a tradition of hard work, perseverance, and thrift, I felt that with faith, determination, and hard work most anything could be accomplished. Those traditions certainly helped me in medical school.

Mormonism is more than a religion; it is a way of life, requiring a great deal of strictness on the part of its members. "The Course of Wisdom is the Course of Obedience," was a pronouncement drilled into my consciousness from earliest childhood. No coffee, tea, tobacco or alcohol was supposed to be used. However, I was never told it was sinful to indulge in these; they just weren't good for me. "How come Grandma drinks coffee and uses snuff?" I often asked. A child's innocent questions are often embarrassing. Nicotine I suppose had become a way of calming her nerves while she worked around the house or in the garden. After all, the use of tobacco wasn't sinful---addictive, but not sinful.

I could certainly see from family experience that drinking alcohol wasn't good. My mother, grandfather, and several cousins had all drunk too much on many occasions. As I grew older the family did lead a more stringent, if not holier life. Mama Parker finally gave up snuff and we switched to decaffeinated coffee. Dad still drank iced tea for many years, but that stopped when Mama Parker died. She had always made him his iced tea and did many other loving things for him, such as ironing and mending his shirts. She had taken care of him as his own mother would have done. They were kind to one another, but did not display much open affection.

We lived in a rural area where there were no other Mormons. Growing up, there definitely was racism within the Mormon Church; however, this was not true of the early church before 1847. Black people were admitted and at least two became priests, Elijah Abel and Walker Lewis, according to *The Changing World of Mormonism* by Jerald and Sandra Tanner. It is only when they migrated to Missouri, a pro-slavery state that Joseph Smith encountered problems. Smith actually ran for president in 1844 on a platform that was gradually to end slavery by 1850. He wanted to sell public lands to buy their freedom.

In 1844 when Brigham Young became president of the Mormon Church, he promoted discriminatory views about black people. In January 1852, he made this pronouncement to the Utah Territorial Legislature stating that

> "If a white man who belongs to the chosen seed mixes his blood with the seed of Cain, the penalty, under the law of God, is death on the spot. This will always be so." (Journal of Discourses, vol. 10, p110). Brigham Young and other church leaders felt that 'one drop of Negro blood' would prevent a person from holding the priesthood.

The idea that Blacks were inferior, and only could be servants to Whites persisted in Mormon theology. Some even seemed to feel that Blacks would still be servants in heaven. According to Joseph Fielding Smith Jr., on August 26, 1908, Joseph Smith, the founder of the Mormon Church, had a Black woman sealed to him as a servant. (Weekly Council Meetings of the Quorum of the Twelve Apostles as printed in *Mormonism-Shadow or Reality,* p 584).

One of the stories told when I was a child was how a Black man was turned White because of his faith in the Mormon Church. Years later, I came to know he suffered from vitiligo, an autoimmune disease which destroys the pigment cells. But to the average Mormon, it was an excellent example of how strict obedience to Mormonism could change anything.

These ideas about Black people being too lazy or cowardly to fight Lucifer in the other world or they were descendants of Cain only helped further prejudices which were present in America at the time I was growing up, especially in the South. Because of this kind of thinking, there were not many Blacks in the Mormon religion at this time.

My grandmother and mother, for instance, had some superstitious beliefs about black people coming to the house on New Year's Day—it was supposed to be bad luck. This had nothing to do with Mormonism and was just some kind of superstition that prevailed in the South and probably other parts of the country as well. I often heard Mother say,

"Well, I've already told Ellie Mae not to show her black ass here tomorrow."

The Southern culture was filled with all kinds of superstitious sayings. They grew out of ignorance and naïveté. We are not born with fear and hate. These emotions are instilled in us by our families, as is prejudice; all created out of fear of the unknown. Perhaps one has to be brought up in a fearful environment and outgrow it—as best one can—to see fear at its most ridiculous: don't hang your clothes on doorknobs; don't lay your hat on a bed; don't walk under ladders, spill salt, sew on Sunday, sing before breakfast ('cause you'll cry before supper), sneeze on Monday (if you do, you'll have bad luck all week), or if you sing at the table, you will marry a crazy woman. These superstitions were inhibiting and emotionally crippling.

My years since leaving home had not been altogether easy, but that's not because of my sneezing on Monday or singing before breakfast. In the battle for existence, one tends to forget unimportant matters, such as superstitions. Superstitions are man's futile, helpless way of saying, almost nostalgically, that he wants things to remain as they are or return to a more embryonic stage of security. They are at best a way of keeping bad luck and change away; and at its worse a withdrawing from the opportunities of life itself. Superstition shows the lack of logical thinking; therefore, a superstitious person fails to think.

Religion itself can be crippling in its extreme forms; this can be said of all faiths at some point in their histories. Instill guilt and people can be controlled in the same way that superstitions control some people. Mankind has always had a weakness for talismans.

To go through the Temple was what every Mormon aspired to do, but none of my family had ever been to one. There weren't any temples in the South at this time, but if a Mormon lived a good life, got a reference from the bishop, it became an earned right to fulfill this holy rite. This meant a journey to one of the Western states, since most of them were in Utah. My mother elected me for this spiritual experience when I was 18 years old. She was struggling for a sense of "wholeness." Mama Parker had died the year before, and I think this had a lot to do with her pushing me toward this celestial goal. Unknowingly, I was really making the journey for my mother.

It was required that I go through the Temple first for myself; afterwards, I stood proxy for my Grandma, so she could be sealed to her parents. Then, she would belong to them in the hereafter and they would "know each other." All Mormons strive to do vicarious works for the dead; they are baptized, married, and given to various families by sealing. These sealing ceremonies assure that a Mormon would be with their relatives in the next life.

This work for the dead often goes back several generations, which explains why the Mormon Church, as a consequence, has one of the largest genealogical institutions in the world. The work that the living members do for their ancestors, offers some unique opportunities for salvation according to church doctrine. If not baptized a Mormon in the flesh while living, there was always, the possibility after death, by proxy. Salvation was offered to those who died without having knowledge of the "truth," but this opportunity often was used by many an exasperated wife who hadn't convinced her husband of the Mormon way of life before his death.

"Work for the dead" was always going on; it was a way to boast modestly of your spirituality by recounting how you had Great-Great Grandpa baptized and married to Great-Great Grandma in the temple. In the ceremonies they always added "for time and all eternity." The Jews brought a lawsuit against the Mormons for this behavior and they no longer baptize those of the Jewish faith into Mormon family trees.

Inconsistencies within Mormonism frequently bothered me even as a child. In Matthew 22, verses 29-33, when Christ was asked to whom would a widowed woman, with more than one husband be given, Jesus answered that in the resurrection, they neither marry nor are they given in marriage, but are as the angels of God in heaven. Although the Mormons don't like to admit it, the divorce rate is increasing among their population, just as it is among the rest of the western world. Temple divorces or annulments are happening in their church just as it is in the Catholic faith and other denominations. Grandpa Parker was married twice, his older son was married three times and the middle son was married two times. Only the youngest of the three sons had one wife.

Since my mother was illegitimate, these various marrying and sealing ceremonies in the temple must have meant a great deal to her. She wanted so much to have her mother married to Willis Parker by the Church so that she would be a legitimate child in the eyes of the family, but most of all in her own eyes. I have often wondered if she knew just exactly who her real father was. Mom suffered another hurt some years later when all the Parkers had her totally eliminated from their family tree, but her half brother, Uncle Earl, was still in the family genealogy. Beatrice remained an orphan all of her life.

After that early visit in the '50s, there had not been much contact between my family and the Parkers over the years. They were closer to Uncle Earl than to us. We exchanged Christmas cards every year, but that was about all. I knew my mother did not like being alienated, and I wondered whether there was more I did not know. I certainly did not feel that I knew them well. Anyway, Mother decided to send my dad and me to Utah. She wanted the Parkers to help me go through the Temple. For me it was a mission into the unknown. For Dad it didn't take a lot to convince him to travel out West. When he was a young man, he had made the journey and looked forward to the adventure of seeing places he had been before, in his younger carefree days. So in 1962, we set out for Salt Lake City in our little Volkswagen and arrived almost as unexpectedly as the Parkers had fourteen years before.

We had appointments at the Manti Temple in southern Utah. My Dad, Grandpa, Zina, and I got up very early to make this pilgrimage. We arrived on time after our 90-minute drive. I must give credit to Zina. She and my grandpa were very helpful in making it possible for me to go to the Temple. It was unusual for a girl of my age to take this initiative, which generally was reserved for people entering into marriage. The commitment was a big one for me, and in many ways I wasn't prepared for what followed. It is surprising that I was allowed to become a temple woman at such a young age, but with persistence many doors can be opened.

The designated Temple attendant, Mr. White, gave me a Patriarchal Blessing. This ceremony was quite long for this solemn occasion, because it would be recorded in the heavens for the angels to look upon and would be a guide, a comfort, and an anchor for my faith.

> *Thou art of the lineage of Ephraim, favored of God, Prince of Israel and the son of Joseph who was sold into Egypt by his brethren. A great work is thine through Ephraim. Thou shall be called upon to do many mighty works for humanity. The Spirit of the Lord would guide thee unto Truth and thou shall fulfill a mighty work.*
>
> *A woman's first great work is to provide tabernacles for the children of men that they might come upon the earth and obtain the training that will help them on to perfection in the plan of 'Life and Salvation'. Furthermore thou must use all*

the intelligence, wisdom, spiritual strength and understanding that can be obtained through faith and right living and study to gain the highest fulfillment of the task for rearing children...

The blessing was one filled with high expectations for my future spouse and me and continued on for at least 15 minutes. One felt sufficiently blessed by the time the Patriarch had finished. Any 18-year old would have been impressed! Now that I am in my 60's, and re-read this blessing, it is still humbling to see what was later typed and sent to me through the mail.

The required garments were the biggest surprise; I didn't realize I was supposed to wear the undergarment all the time. At the ceremony I was ritually washed, anointed with holy oil and dressed in the temple garments. It was one piece that covered the torso, the thighs and had an open crotch. There were geometric symbols embroidered over the nipple area, the navel and over the right knee. These symbols served as a reminder of the temple ceremonies and of the potential sacredness of our own bodies as the temples of the Holy Spirit. The garment was a protection against evil and a symbol of one's faithfulness to the Church.

After I had received my endowments (blessing), as the initial anointing ceremony is called, I joined my Grandpa and Zina to proceed through the temple. We sat in various beautifully appointed rooms, decorated with elaborate wall murals of the earth's creation and listened to dramatic readings over the public address system. In order to pass from one of the three main rooms to the other, certain hand grips and secret passwords were taught to be repeated. A large veil of sheer, voile-like material served as a room divider, separating the "passer" from the "door keeper," and the hands were gripped through special openings in the veil. When the correct information had been given, a section of the veil was parted, to let the initiates pass through. Sometimes, a hundred or more people passed through at a session. It was time-consuming; therefore, even though five or six people were accommodated at the veil at one time, the whole ceremony must have taken us four hours. Since I was a new initiate, it took a bit longer than usual for me. The initiation alone must have taken an hour. My new name was Esther. Zina asked me what name I was given; she wondered if every one got the same name for that day. She inquired and this was apparently the case.

Except for the undergarment, it had been possible for me to rent the temple outfit. Of course, Grandpa and Zina had their own clothes, but coming ill-equipped as I did, it was a good thing this rental service was available. The complete outfit with white stockings, tunic, green apron, bonnet-tams for the men, seemed to me to be a combination between a pilgrim's and a Scottish Highlander's costume. I had never seen any attire like it before, nor have I since! The apron was supposed to be a representation of Adam's fig leaf and was so shaped. We started our journey through the temple with the simple white clothing and white shoes; then we progressed from room to room, putting on various other pieces of clothing, that we carried, i.e., the tunic, the tam or bonnet and the apron. At one point toward the end, we all joined hands with the rest of the group and danced around in a circle.

The doctrine of three degrees of glory is not in harmony with the teachings of the Book of Mormon, according to Jerald and Sandra Tanner. In 1 Nephi 15:35 only heaven and hell are mentioned: "And there is a place prepared, yea, even that awful hell of which I have spoken, and the devil is the foundation of it; wherefore the final state of the souls of men is to dwell in the kingdom of God, or to be cast out because of that justice of which I have spoken."

The Temple ceremony centers around three main rooms representing the three kingdoms of heaven: the telestial, the terrestrial, and the celestial that were likened unto the stars, the moon and the sun in terms of spiritual attainment. "Those who reject the gospel, but live honorable lives, shall also be heirs of salvation, but not in the celestial kingdom. The Lord has prepared a place for them in the terrestrial kingdom. Those who live lives of wickedness may be heirs of salvation but they were relegated to the telestial kingdom (Doctrines of Salvation, vol.2, p 133).

The material wealth of each chamber changed accordingly to signify its brightness and worth and the final one was a great hall, resplendent with deep carpeting, wall hangings, crystal chandeliers, and beautifully upholstered pieces of furniture. It was the most like a palace of splendor, unlike any place I had ever seen. Of course, it was the celestial kingdom.

At the end of the Temple ceremony, Grandpa, Zina and I had a special sealing rite performed. They stood proxy for Mama Parker's parents, the Holsworths, and I stood proxy for my maternal grandmother. Mama Parker was sealed to them for eternity. This sealing really was the culmination of it all; and looking back, I can see this function had been Mother's goal all along. Of course, what she would have liked even better was the marriage of Grandpa to Mama Parker in the temple with her being sealed to them. She would have gained a real sense of belonging, a legitimacy which she badly needed. On the other hand, it might not have had any effect. After all, she herself didn't have the courage to go through the Temple for her own endowments; she would have needed a man for this at her age. The Mormon Church probably would not have allowed it and in retrospect, it is surprising that they allowed me. Beatrice was simply fraught with too many doubts and fears about her own life. Her feelings toward her mother remained ambivalent and unresolved. Having me go through the Temple may have been her "one-upmanship" to impress her stepfather and perhaps her half brother, Uncle Earl. However, Earl stayed on the periphery of the Mormon Church, partly because Aunt Bertha had been a Jehovah's Witness. They mostly attended the Baptist Church.

My dad waited patiently for us while we completed this mission. I really don't remember what he did while we were busy purifying our souls and anointing our bodies, but he was there for us when we came out. He was his usual amiable self.

We went farther West when we said good-bye to Utah. Dad enjoyed visiting the Bonneville Salt Flats, and we had a day in the Great Salt Lake, the lake where you cannot sink because it is so salty. We also had been corresponding with the oldest of the Parkers three sons who lived in California, so we traveled to San Francisco to spend a few days with his family. Since Dad wanted to see the Golden Gate Bridge, we had a picnic in the park overlooking the bridge. I don't remember much else about the visit. They were cordial to us and treated us as family. Everybody loved to talk with my dad. He could be very agreeable and I loved to travel with him.

We had some car trouble on the way back in Albuquerque, New Mexico. The alternator in the Volkswagen went bad. After this was repaired, the drive home was much better. Dad always enjoyed telling everyone how little gas the VW had used for this coast-to-coast journey.

When Dad and I returned from our trip to Utah, my mother was depressed and withdrawn. We didn't know exactly what her trouble was. Her "nerves were bad" and we knew she'd been running from doctor to doctor looking for some help. We thought it would pass, but at times it seemed hopeless. She seemed to go downhill after the death of her mother, grieving a lot, not eating well, and turning to tranquilizers to escape. Many doctors in the area were only too willing to write prescriptions for an aging postmenopausal woman. Not one of them would take the time to sit and talk to her, and attempt to sort out the root of her "bad nerves."

Mother hadn't been drinking in years; in fact, the period in which she did drink to excess probably was no more than a year. It had seemed longer to me because it had produced so much discord in our lives. To see Mom under the influence of alcohol or drugs was always frightening for me. Her personality changed during these times; I was petrified. We always knew when she had been indulging in prescription drugs by the look in her eyes. The sparkle would leave her eyes and they would become somnolent and indifferent. Then, I missed her usual warmth. She could be such a great friend, filled with lots of energy and vitality.

Regrettably, the Temple ceremony had not been what I had expected in terms of spiritual awakening; it had been only a ritual for me. For a long time I thought something was wrong with me and experienced some guilt about it all. I knew I'd have to learn to wear those undergarments. That thought alone took some getting used to. In general, the garment actually was comfortable, except for the open crotch—I had to remember to be careful when I sat down. Also some of the cheaper materials had a way of creeping up your leg. I had bought four pieces of underwear, at Zina's suggestion, and found the more expensive nylon was the best buy. She also said the garments should be washed by hand. The attire was a lifetime commitment to remain a Mormon in good standing. I have more recently read books written by Mormon missionaries and today the garment is no longer one piece, rather more like a T-shirt with a long legged brief. Modern times required changes.

My dad had stayed in the background during all the spiritualization. He wasn't the kind of person with whom I could seriously discuss such matters. He had a practical sense of humor, and I suspect, a way of closing his mind to what he couldn't understand. One of his favorite sayings was, "I'm not pleasing everybody, but everyone isn't pleasing me." It carried a sad, deeper meaning than I realized.

Whatever sexual awakenings there might normally have stirred in me, were dampened by this journey to "Mecca." I was a virgin at 18 and would remain one until I was 23 years old. I planned to save myself for the right man, probably a Mormon or one who would understand all this garment business. As it turned out, the right man did not come along and it never occurred to me at this time, to ever take the undergarment off. Perhaps this had been a way my mother tried to control me—a manipulation. Of course, knowing what I do now, I can see how Mama Parker's getting pregnant out of wedlock and Mother having an affair, may have caused her to fear what I might do. Nevertheless, it was a useful brainwashing for a young woman, and to be a temple woman placed my life on an untenable course.

It was the best of times, it was the worst of times, it was the season of Light, it was the season of Darkness, it was the spring of Hope, it was the winter of Despair.

Charles Dickens

Chapter Four
Poetry

From my mother I developed a great love of literature and poetry. She taught me a number of poems, and I remember some of them to this day. She could still recite them when she was 80 years old. The first one I learned was:

When I grow up I'm going to be
The sweetest girl you ever did see;
I'll wash the dishes and sweep the floor,
And if I can I'll do something more;
I'll not quarrel and tattle and fight,
Like most girls do every night.
I'll just speak in a gentle tone.

I'll just be wonderful when I'm grown.
But Mother says she cannot see
When that big change is going to be;
If I'm going to do anything at all,
I'd better begin while I'm small.

Author unknown

Another one of her favorites was a poem about thinking.

It's just a little thing to do,
Just to think.
Anyone, no matter who,
Ought to think.
Take a little time each day
From the moments thrown away.
Spare it from your work or play.
Men who find themselves in jail,
Do not think.
  Half the trouble buried for you and me
Perhaps it would never be if we'd think.
  Now shall we journey
Hit or miss, rather than to ourselves confess.
It would help us more or less
If we'd think.

Author unknown

I was an avid reader and Charles Dickens, Victor Hugo, and Jane Austen were some of my favorite authors. They told stories that were more of an escape for me than the movies. These stories were of the poor and downtrodden who somehow rose above their circumstances and had a happy ending, such as *Oliver Twist, David Copperfield, Great Expectations, Jane Eyre, The Tale of Two Cities,* and *Les Miserable.*

Reciting poems was an important part in the Mormon Church as well as sermons or testimonials. My mother probably learned many poems when she went on a Mormon mission to Tampa, Florida. One of her favorite poems that she was able to recite well into her 80th decade of life sounded like a mission poem:

Throw wide your gates
Ye ballon tree.
Let music from your song
Float out on every breeze
To thrill with joy each living thing.
Behold this message from the King:
The arch is wide,
Go through and teach the
Remnant of this land,
The prophecy is to understand.
And His word is not in vain,
But his covenant is sure.
Redemption calls,
Sweet mercy pleads,
Oh, would you rise to endure.

Author unknown

Her recitations were always filled with such passion and she could be quite dramatic. Her passionate words of endurance and perseverance sustained me many times. Beatrice shared not only poetry but her love of French stayed with me. She only knew a few phrases but she passed them on to me. It was something she couldn't share with my father because his formal education ended in the eighth grade. However, he was an intelligent man who learned from life and graduated from the University of Hard Knocks.

My mother seemingly did not always learn from life; she had an independent spirit, was headstrong, and articulate. She existed in her own world. Maybe she was more of a daydreamer, which eventually became a mental illness. She could have tried to share her world with my father, but he was far too practical by nature. He was busy making a living—caught on the treadmill of life that we all get on unknowingly in supporting a family. As long as my mother had some creative outlet she seemed to thrive. My dad was a farm boy who spit, picked his nose because he didn't know there were tissues. Unfortunately with ten children in his family handkerchiefs would have been quite a luxury and too much bother to wash. Kleenex did not exist at this time, at least not in their world.

Beatrice had aspirations of rising above where we were; she didn't just want money and the numerous things it could buy, she was striving for respectability. We were not part of the upper crust. She wanted to learn how to act in different situations. Now I realize she had an inferiority complex and this often manifested itself as arrogance. I remember her saying,

"Well, I bet your cousin Willis has told his mother how to act."

Telling a 14 or 15 year old such things were enigmas that could not be sorted out. A child does not often second-guess a parent. Some of Mother's comments to me still remain a mystery.

Sometimes in order to make herself feel better, she would point out imagined flaws in me. Once when we were at the beach she said, "Look you have a space between your thighs when you put your legs together, mine have no space."

Well, I now know that she had cellulite and her thighs were too large, mine were just right for my age and size. As a small child I didn't understand. She was sensitive to looks and status. As time went by she didn't age gracefully. Perhaps some of her inferiorities went back to her early childhood and may even have been generational. A biblical verse that I read in a Sunday school lesson reminded me of generational bitterness. "Sour grapes eaten by parents (and grandparents) leave a bitter taste in the mouths of their children." (Jeremiah 31:29)

Gone with the Wind was next to the Bible in many Southern homes. It, of course, is an epic tale that glamorized what life was like before, during, and after the Civil War. In the South, some in the farmer class were trying to make it to the plantation status and they, in turn, were trying to get to the planter status. Each rung on the ladder required more land and more slaves to advance socially. Some planters had as many as several thousand slaves. According to Bruce Levine's book *The Fall of the House of Dixie*, many of the Confederate policies of Jefferson Davis generated class resentment among sectors of the white majority who had no slaves. The planters were the most elite group in the Old South. The planter class was also released from serving in the Confederate Army. It didn't take long for the "volunteer" who had no slaves to figure out they were fighting for the rich man's Negro. Therefore, the ravages of the Civil War still weighed heavily on the rural South as I was growing up.

I was born less than 100 years after the Civil War, but to Mama Parker, both the war and class were still very real. She always made me feel that we were better than anyone else, and from my earliest recollections this attitude of hers began with the Yankees, and then filtered down to the "white trash" in our part of the county. I grew up with stories of how life had been at her home in Wilkinson County and how the Yankees pillaged their home during the War Between the States—it was never referred to as the Civil War! Sometimes a Southerner might smile and call it the War of Northern Aggression! A small child of the family was even supposedly kidnapped and never heard from again. My grandmother was born on June 29, 1890, so she wasn't old enough to know if the stories were true. I don't know if she ever questioned them, nor did I, until I was much older. Her father and mother had come from North Carolina to Georgia and reared their family there. They had five surviving children, three girls and two boys; my grandmother was the eldest daughter.

As I was growing up, Northerners were called Yankees. What was a Yankee to us? They were from the North and were generally driving through Georgia on their way to Florida, escaping the cold weather. These people almost always took the same route south every winter, and the southern sheriffs began to look out for them. Interstate 95 didn't exist yet. Speed traps became notorious for these "snowbirds", and word got around where to be careful. Ludowici, Georgia was an especially infamous location. If trophies had been given to the sheriff for catching the most Yankees, the Sheriff of Ludowici certainly would have stayed in first place!

For the most part, critical and demanding people were foreign to the Southerner. "Southern Gentleman" came from the slow, gentle ways of the fellows. Even after a hundred years since the Civil War, their slow speech was considered by some Northerners as a sign of slowness of thinking. To this day, the Civil War occupies a major and powerfully emotional place in the Southern folk memory—to many it seems as though it happened just a decade ago. As an unknown author once said, *there is great power in letting go, and there is great freedom in moving on.*

Many times I heard the stories about the terrible havoc General Sherman unleashed on the South, especially on Georgia. According to Bruce Levine's book on the Civil War, Sherman hoped this horrible destruction would break the South's will to continue the war. In his march to the seacoast of Savannah, Sherman himself estimated that his men destroyed $100,000,000 worth of property in Georgia. People are still outraged to this day. My mother would not go to a doctor by the name of Sherman and when her family doctor insisted that she go, one of the first things she asked was,

"Is he related to General Sherman?" This was during the later half of the 1980's!

The Southerners had a tongue-in-cheek way of talking about reconstruction. I thought carpetbaggers, the opportunistic Northerners who made their money off the whipped Southerners, were "carpet beggars" until I was in my twenties. Then I learned these opportunists carried all their belongings in carpetbags. Most were looking for financial rewards. Reconstruction is never an easy task, but if there had been a strong leader in the North to shape the post war policies such as General Marshall of WWII, the recovery of the South would have been faster and much less painful. Had Lincoln lived, he probably would have stemmed the tide of opportunism and exploitation that the South experienced. The prejudice of the Southerners and Northerners would probably be much less than it is today, more than a hundred fifty years later.

There were no plantations in our family. As far as I know, we did not have anyone in the social aristocracy associated with such enterprises. Prior to the Civil War, Georgia's Governor Hugh Fitzhugh had proclaimed that the white men of the South came from a master race. With such ideas promoted from a man in a high position, it is little wonder that Southern Gentlemen were so arrogant and fathered so many children with the Negro women on their plantations. Slaves were of great economic value and the more children they fathered, the greater the owners' wealth. The slave owners had a ruthless way of thinking.

The Southerners fought the Civil War to preserve this unfair system and the slaves and the poor whites suffered great losses from this ill conceived "glorious war." As a young person, I would hear declarations that the reason the Civil War was fought had more to do with states rights and opposition of a central government. Of course, Lincoln wanted to preserve the Union at all costs; he was not going

At the Crossroads: A Southern Daughter's Story

to let the South secede. According to *The Fall of the House of Dixie* by Bruce Levine, by the end of the war a third to a half of the Confederate army had deserted, and more than 300,000 Southern whites were fighting for the Union.

That fact helps me to understand the letter my great, great grandfather wrote about sensing some danger. From the letter,* it sounds as if he didn't want to be conscripted into a rich man's war that was all but over. Like me, my grandmother was quite the archivist and she had saved his letters for a century before she gave them to me, the newly appointed archivist.

*He had written on March 5, 1865, from Mobile, Alabama:

> "My dear Sisters Carolyn and Martha,
> I again take the privilege of writing you a few lines, hoping they will reach you both and find you well. I have nothing very new or interesting to tell; I am in good health and have avoided or kept out of the war up to the present time and I think I will continue to keep out. I was in Macon some two weeks since and intended to visit you but apprehending some danger, I declined doing so until some more favorable opportunity arrives. Miss Bowman's written to you during my absence something to this affect...[he did not elaborate].
>
> We are expecting the Yankees to take this city every day. I am still living with Mrs. Price, a very nice lady indeed. She has moved to this city instead of going to Pensacola as I before wrote you. I am making shoes and getting along as good as could be desired. We live near the center of town that is three miles square.

Provisions are very high: corn meal $20 per bushel, flour $500 per barrel, Bacon $3 a pound, eggs are $6 a dozen and wood is $60 to $80 a cord with everything else in proportion.

Give my best to all your children and to Henry and all who inquire of me and also present the same to my little children. Tell them I will see them in better days if I live.

May God bless you both with families and friends with love and happy lives is the sincere prayer of your affectionate and relieved brother,

Meredith Holsworth.
P.S. Direct your letters to Miss A.K. Bowens, Mobile, Alabama."

Because of the desertion among the ranks of the Confederacy, there was a feeling of general lawlessness during this time. People were fearful of strangers and always had their guns to protect their property or person. Reconstruction only added to problems in the South. Freeing the slaves and giving land to the blacks who had no education or sense about making a living was worthless. These factors lead to tenant farming. Many people define this period as a type of serfdom, but it was the only way the poor whites and blacks could survive. Not having grown up in this era, I have no first hand knowledge; however, I remember the Jim Crow times.

We lived at the Crossroads where three different families had corners; my family had two, but heard stories of how Great Grandpa Holsworth had owned it all when he first settled in the County. He had five children, and when they inherited their piece of land some of them sold out to the Joneses and a family by the name of Rice. Some of the relatives of the five children settled in North Carolina but always managed to return to their roots and visit Mama Parker, my grandmother, who was their aunt and their father's oldest sister. We had many extended relatives visit during her lifetime.

We lived on a hill and the Joneses and the Rices lived about 600 yards away on their respective corners. Each family had three children: two boys and a girl and they were all about the same ages. The older children were busy with work or school, but I played cowboys and Indians with the youngest boy and the two youngest girls. We built imaginary houses with boards and sawhorses that were available on the farm, and made mud pies out of dirt and water. We also had a homemade swing put together from rope and a board on which to sit; it was strung over a large branch of the pecan tree. I loved to swing and feel the wind in my hair.

It was also fun playing with Laurie, who was Ellie Mae's granddaughter. Laurie spent a lot of time with Ellie Mae during the summer while her mother Marie worked in Savannah. I also spent a great deal of time alone, creating my own world or practicing my music or dance lessons. Mother was determined to make something of me! She never missed a chance to try to cultivate talent if any sign appeared.

One summer, while Mother was attending classes to finish her college degree, I took voice lessons at the Teachers' College in Statesboro. That happened because we had seen the Firestone Hour on TV, and I imitated Jeannette Nelson singing *If I Could Tell You*, in my musical routine. I'm also told that in my most mature 10-year-old voice, I had tried to sing opera. As a result of these fantasies, my mother arranged voice lessons for me to take during the summer; I learned to sing *The Sweetest Story Ever Told*.

When the summer course work ended, so did the voice lessons; but the piano lessons continued, followed by four years of tap dancing and ballet.

Mother used to say, "Joan, I want you to be well-rounded." And so, in the name of "well-roundedness" among other things, Mother and I left the farm and went to the city when I was nine.

The first line of the lyrics of *The Sweetest Story Ever Told* was "Tell me that you love me." I was asked to perform this more than once for various family members who came to visit, especially those who came from North Carolina. It always embarrassed me to have to do this, but I sang nonetheless. I felt as if Mother was trying to make me into a Shirley Temple, whose movies were popular with my mother's age group. In addition, many of our visitors had girls my age who were quite accomplished. I always felt as if our mothers were just putting us on display.

Our relatives from North Carolina generally visited in the summers, when the children were out of school. My grandmother was fond of her widowed sister-in-law, as well as her boys. The feeling was mutual and they liked to return to the familiar places of their childhood. They often brought Mama Parker fancy dishes trimmed in gold, which were safely stored away and never used.

One of Mama Parker's nephews worked in a North Carolina textile industry where he grew quite wealthy by our standards. He flew his own airplane, and sometimes he would even fly his family down to a nearby airport for a weekend visit. However, they always stayed in a motel. I'll never forget the thrill of riding in his airplane—another first adventure for me.

During World War II, my grandmother and mother had been made the guardian of a little girl who was a great niece of my grandmother's and was related to the family in North Carolina. Her name was Maggie and they talked many times about her as I was growing up. Maggie's mother was from the local community but she had been caught "running around" while Maggie's dad, a local hero was serving in Japan. He was one of the soldiers who had survived the Bataan Death March. His daughter was described to me as having dimples and curly hair, so they thought she looked like Shirley Temple. My mother and Mama Parker often talked about her and all the "cute" things she would say. I wasn't sure what to make of their conversations. Did Maggie represent what they wanted me to be? I was so young at this time, but I do remember being jealous when they talked about her.

While Maggie's father was serving in the U.S. Army in Japan and becoming a prisoner of war, he received word that his wife was seeing another man and had become pregnant with him.

When he came home, he divorced his wife, who by this time had children by another man, and took his daughter to live with him in North Carolina. He eventually married the widow of a buddy from the Bataan Death March. He was one of the thousands of American and Philippinos captured by the Japanese in World War II and forced to march 80 miles in the Philippines. They were murdered, abused, and tortured; and thousands died along the way from Bataan to Capas. [In May 2009, the Japanese government formally apologized through its ambassador in the USA to the few surviving American prisoners of war.]

The North Carolina relatives came frequently to visit my family and I finally got to know Maggie better. She was no longer a figment of my imagination. She was five or six years older than I, had red curly hair and freckles—a regular Shirley Temple.

The woods are lovely, dark and deep,
But I have promises to keep,
And miles to go before I sleep,
And miles to go before I sleep.

Robert Frost

Chapter Five
Medical School

I started college at Emory at Oxford College, a 4-year prep school. It was a small campus, a satellite of Emory University in Atlanta with an excellent reputation. My Uncle Earl, who was a county school superintendent, recommended it to my mom and dad and that is primarily why I went. Students could do their last two years of high school and two years of college there. It was rather expensive and probably beyond my family's budget, so I only went there just one year. Many of the students were from well-to-do families from Atlanta; I particularly remember the Coca Cola and Chandler newspaper heirs. Everyone was in a socially engaging sport like golf or tennis, as well as the mind-challenging games of chess or bridge, which were all foreign to me.

This was my first exposure to the Methodist Church because Emory was founded by the Methodists. I sang in the choir and went to the evening vespers. We had regular school assemblies like the ones in British boarding schools as seen on television. Besides being enrolled in the college pre-med program, I was introduced to classical Greek and Roman cultures.

At Mount Vernon High I had written few term papers, so was ill prepared for some of the humanities assignments. To my surprise, instead of being the top student in the class, I found I was just average to slightly below average. This was a blow to my ego.

The first semester was difficult, making me even more homesick; consequently, a ten-pound weight loss was experienced during this period. The sadness must have shown on my face, because several of the girls started calling me "Sunshine." There were many letters written to my folks complaining about being homesick. A "sleepover" at my high school classmate's house was about as far away from home as I had ever been, only occasionally visiting relatives with my family. My parents did not encourage my going on the senior trip to NYC and I don't remember protesting, having become accustomed to being cocooned. This is why transitioning to college was so hard.

I did finally toughen up and the next year transferred to the University of Georgia. The tuition fees were much less at the state university, which was good for my family. Life in the dormitory wasn't so bad, if you had a good roommate. Emory at Oxford placed three girls in a room, so two students had to sleep in a bunk bed. Never having slept in a bunk bed, I had a fear of falling out. Finally, I got the bottom bunk. Such are the hardships of a freshman's life at college. One had to also endure criticism from one's peers; it was the first time I realized I slurped my tea—drawing in air while sipping my beverage. My roommates pointed out this annoying habit right away and I was suitably mortified.

It was my second year of college and I was still in the pre-med program. The University of Georgia was huge in comparison to Emory at Oxford and my graduating class in 1964 had over 2000 students. The dormitories were modern and convenient to most of my classes. I shared a room with another girl, who was quite pleasant; it was definitely an improvement over the old dorms at the previous college. We had a kitchen and a recreation room with a television and I got hooked on some afternoon soap operas. One was "The Edge of Night" with a woman who suffered with alcoholism. The soaps were addictive but something to look forward to every day—other people's dramas. Many others joined me in the television room; this became a common practice among many college students, a chance to escape from the routine of our studies.

Going to summer school every term enabled me to finish four years of college in three years. A normal course load was usually 15 hours per quarter, but my average was 20 to 22 credits. Today, studying for any advanced education has become such an enterprise; a student does well to finish a course of study in four years. It takes careful planning to beat the system at most colleges and universities.

Being the child of a teacher can be difficult because teachers like to keep their children busy. As a high school student, I was enrolled in French one summer and Latin the following year. This was not offered locally, so it meant my living about two hours away from home; my mother found me a room in a house off campus. Naturally, after entering medical school, I found some work during the summer. Only this time, a stipend was included for the study. This was a welcome surprise.

The work was at the Pathology Department with Dr. Puchtlar, a German research professor, specializing in chemical stains for tissue pathology. She was the first European I had ever met and was most hospitable. Standing not an inch over 4' 8", she always wore high-wedge heels to make her look taller. She often invited students to her apartment and offered us a glass of sherry and conversation. There were many coffee table books on baroque culture that seemed like a fairy tale to me.

With her I made my first trip to Baltimore to give a presentation. Because she did not like to fly, we took the train from Augusta to Baltimore. This was the first time I traveled by train. What an experience! Several other medical students went along. Even though we all had sleeping berths, it was all too exciting to sleep. Later the Medical College of Georgia sent me to the AFIP (Armed Forces Institute of Pathology) and the NIH (National Institute of Health) for another learning experience. Both of the Institutes are located in Washington, D. C.

I was by no means the smartest student in my class, so I felt honored to be singled out for these programs. All Department Heads encourage medical students to enter into their field of study, so I was coddled a bit in the Pathology Department. All my years at testimony meetings as a Mormon made me a better speaker than most of my classmates. In those Mormon services, members were expected to stand and give thanks for the Mormon Church and the Gospel of Jesus Christ. Then the members gave examples of how their lives changed or how they had witnessed for the Church to other people. Actually, I had grown up without knowing I was doing the course work for Public Speaking 101. Therefore, I had acquired the gift to speak authoritatively once I understood the subject.

After one of my trips sponsored by the Medical College of Georgia, Dr. Stockman, the chief of the department approached me and said, "Miss Joan, I want you to get all your notes together on the conference while they are fresh in your mind for our seminar presentation."

I spoke about my experience with enthusiasm. It had been a great experience to go to Washington, D.C.; the city itself was overwhelming for a country girl. The days started quite early because we had to catch the bus at 7AM to arrive at the conference by 7:30 and the lectures started by 7:45. Various subjects were discussed by researchers and we visited many laboratories. The impressive National

Library of Medicine was located at the National Institute of Health. The information shared in those days before much computerization was mind-boggling. One of the doctors gave a lecture on Tumor Viruses in Tissue Culture. This was cutting edge research in 1966. The data processing center was amazing and was the type of work I was doing for the Department of Pathology—coding and computers were to become the bane of our existence.

I had read a book by Dr Howard Hobbs and it was exciting to get to meet him. Dr. Hobbs had written about Geographic Pathology and I had found it fascinating. He discussed how customs and geographic locations of people can cause certain diseases. Other speakers lectured on the embryology of the heart with its various anomalies.

As a second year medical student, such topics as x-ray diffraction and fluorescent studies were intellectually stimulating. The diffraction was particularly interesting. Specimens from the laboratory that appeared to have pigment within them, as from a mole or birthmark, were analyzed and subsequently found to be an entirely different material. With the new technique of chemical staining of tissue, diffraction solved the mystery.

A forensic pathologist could prove that the substance was perhaps barium sulfate or some other chemical, and not pigment. Then the question arose—from where did the substance come? It was like a Sherlock Holmes mystery. What a wonderful opportunity I had been given!

The following summer I was offered a job in the Surgical Pathology Department and Dr. Petersen became my mentor; he originally came from Stuttgart and had been recruited as a professor for the medical school. He had a reputation for being a womanizer in spite of his wife and two boys. I knew he had a girlfriend because I had seen an attractive blonde-haired woman visiting him on many occasions. This gave rise to some of the usual idle gossip that goes on at any institution.

Anyway, I found him pleasant and conversation was easy with him, although he was my senior by ten to fifteen years. I shared things about my life and Dr. Petersen reminisced with me about his early experiences in Germany.

His family had some connections with the original *Eau de Cologne* factory and chemical industry. One of his forebears came from Koeln and the cologne was named after his ancestor's hometown, which means cologne in English. The fragrance *4711* is probably one of the oldest and best known in the world, having a distinct citrus scent; at one time a small bottle cost a fortune. The production formula of *4711* began in 1709 and its distinctive homogeneous scent comprising dozens of citrus essences remains a well-kept secret to this day. Dr. Petersen's family apparently had amassed considerable wealth before WWII.

I accompanied him to the State Mental Hospital in Millegeville where he was their consulting pathologist. I told him about Harry on one of our hour-long drives and he became unusually short with me. He said, "You little fool that boy really cared for you." I said, "Yes, I know he did, but I was not sure I could marry a non-Christian and make a marriage work." Then he threw a bombshell at me saying, "Some people think Jesus was a schizophrenic and just recently a book about this has been published." Then he added, "You know my grandmother was Jewish."

Some weeks later, I threw him a bombshell. "That blonde-haired lady who frequently visits your office, I think she's just a younger version of your wife. Why are you trying to recapture your youth with this younger woman?" We always had an unusual exchange!

I learned a lot from him especially about "seeing" correctly. Dr. Petersen would get a surgical pathology specimen and have me describe it—size, color, texture etc... He bashed some of my observations and conclusions. One day I had to describe an unusual specimen—an amputated penis with a large carcinoma, and he asked me why I thought this man had developed cancer?

I said, "There is some speculation that being uncircumcised can lead to cancer."

Well, Petersen replied, "I've still got my foreskin and I intend to keep it." [I later read that viruses, immunity, moisture and cleanliness play more significant roles in carcinoma of the penis than circumcision.]

All this experience still did not lure me into becoming a pathologist. I enjoyed interacting with people too much to sit in front of a microscope and read tissue pathology, deal with laboratory equipment, as well as do autopsies on dead bodies. My first love was dermatology and it stayed with me. Art had also been one of my first loves. I enjoyed drawing and did many watercolors in my spare time. Dermatology was a visual discipline of medicine and I knew I wanted to study it more than any other field.

Even though many women had been admitted to medical schools, we were still somewhat of a novelty. The men were not really gentlemen; they were still adolescent in much of their behavior in the anatomy lab. Not too long after we began the dissection of the body, one of those adolescents placed a tongue in the vagina of the cadaver as a joke. They were at times downright vulgar, with very little respect for the human body. One fellow student asked, "Any ideas why my girlfriend's tampon only gets blood on one side?" Then they would laugh like idiots!

> My anatomy professor whispered a Latin phrase to me, "illegitimi non carborundum" translating its meaning, "Don't let the bastards grind you down."

I had many champions early on as I look back. The pathology professors were also good mentors and encouraged women. I wish I had felt at liberty to give them big hugs. The whole experience of being in medicine was grueling and not for the faint of heart. You had to have tenacity—true grit! I had it and was determined, but at times felt as if I might have an emotional breakdown. It helped that "I kept my head about me, when everyone else was losing theirs" to paraphrase Kipling. I was young, studious and not sexually active; this got me through the years. I graduated shortly before turning 24 years of age. Rudyard Kipling's poem "IF," which Kipling wrote for his son, was my inspiration and a beacon for my life, even to this day.

If you can keep your head when all about you
Are losing theirs and blaming it on you;
If you can trust yourself when all men doubt you,
But make allowance for their doubting too.
If you can wait and not be tired by waiting,
Or, being lied about, don't deal in lies,
Or, being hated don't give way to hating,
And yet don't look too good, nor talk too wise.

If you can dream-and not make dreams your master;
If you can think—and not make thoughts your aim,
If you can meet with Triumph and Disaster
And treat those two imposters just the same;
If you can bear to hear the truth you've spoken
Twisted by knaves to make a trap for fools,
Or watch the things you gave your life to, broken,
And stoop and build 'em up with worn-out-tools;
If you can make one heap of all your winnings
And risk it on one turn of pitch-and-toss,
And lose, and start again at your beginnings,
And never breathe a word about your loss:

At the Crossroads: A Southern Daughter's Story

If you can force your head and nerve and sinew
To serve your turn long after they are gone,
And so hold on when there is nothing in you
Except the Will which says to them: "Hold on!"

If you can talk with crowds and keep your virtue,
Or walk with Kings--nor lose the common touch,
If neither foes nor loving friends can hurt you,
If all men count with you, but none too much:
If you can fill the unforgiving minute
With sixty seconds' worth of distance run,
Yours is the Earth and everything that's in it,
And—what's more—you'll be a Man, my son!

During my first year of medical school, I lived in the nurse's dormitory. There were some apartments on campus and I applied for one of them the following year. The basic apartments had 4 small bedrooms, and an open floor plan of a kitchen and living room plus a bathroom with shower. It was an improvement over the nurse's dorm, where the showers and toilets were down a corridor.

One of my roommates announced her engagement during her second year. She was dating a Jewish medical student, a year ahead of her. Since she was converting to Judaism most of her spare time was spent with him or going to Hebrew school on the weekends. They were also avid tennis players. A second roommate married the following year.

When my roommates married and moved out I got new ones. One girl was particularly chipper and spunky. She introduced me to horseback riding. I learned how to canter and do some jumping but became too busy to pursue the sport for any length of time. Besides, it was beyond my budget. Nevertheless, the experience gave me a window into another world.

One of my more interesting roommates was a biochemist who was working on her PhD. She had a terrific sense of humor, could swear and drink like a sailor and was also a chain smoker. Unfortunately she suffered from depression at times, and it got so bad at one point she consented to electro-shock treatment. There weren't as many pharmaceutical anti-depressants in the late '60s as there are today. The electro-shock treatment helped the depression but it changed her personality. Although no longer depressed, her sparkle had disappeared.

During my senior year, I started sharing my meals with some guys in an apartment across the courtyard. I was in a study group with one of them and we were all in the same class. We took turns shopping, cooking and cleaning up and split the costs four ways. I often brought steaks from the farm and the homegrown beef was quite a treat for all of us. We became really good buddies and I remain thankful for them. I felt honored to be one of the "Guys." Many of us remained good friends until we married and got busier with our own lives.

Toward the latter half of my senior year of medical school, I did a rotation through the newly founded Department of Dermatology. The attitude of the new chairman toward women was appalling. As I chatted informally with him one afternoon, he said, "Training women is not worthwhile, because they marry and require too much time off for their families." Quickly I replied, "But they generally have longer careers."

It was sad to hear such comments out of the mouth of an educated man. I never bothered to send in an application for his program; he was simply too chauvinistic for me.

I might have remained a virgin had it not been for a second year medical student, who had purchased some used textbooks from me and subsequently asked me out. He was from Ohio, had soulful brown eyes, was a good listener and played the guitar. We had no burning romance, however, curiosity got the best of me, and he was my first "official" sexual encounter. There was no one I had been "saving" myself for. I had engaged in some petting, but something was always amiss with the men in my social circle. My lab partner and friend since pre-med days was a horrible kisser; he had thin lips and always did this passionate French kissing that was just awful. A soft gentle kiss was more welcome. I was not to find my ultimate dream kisser for some years.

We receive love from our children as well as others, not in proportion to our demands or sacrifices or needs, but roughly in proportion to our own capacity to love.

Rollo May

Chapter Six
Remembering Dad

My dad had been a handsome man and was still attractive in middle age. I had seen a photograph of his standing by his first car in a suit with a vest—tall and slender with black wavy hair and a neatly trimmed moustache. He and my mother had been married in the fall of 1937, when he was 26 and she was 24, but it was seven years before I was born. Dad was the second oldest of ten children, and he had many responsibilities for the younger children. Perhaps, that explains why they waited so long to have children.

Mother told me all about how they both had looked forward to my coming into the world. When her water broke, she said my dad was plowing in a field. They drove 30 miles to Macon where I was born at the hospital in June of 1944 I weighed 11 lbs, so I had to be delivered by C-Section. My dad was a man of few words, but I'm told his first words were, "She looks just like me!"

I never sensed any disappointment in the family that I was a girl rather than a boy, but they did nickname me "Baby Boy," because I didn't have much hair in the early years. The

"Boy" was dropped, but to my dad I always remained "Baby" until I finished medical school.

My given name was Elmere Joan Johnson after my dad. "Elmere" was the feminine form of my father's first name, Elmer. I carried that name on my diplomas from high school, University of Georgia, and later the Medical College of Georgia. Finally, I discretely dropped the Elmere and became E. Joan Johnson. I had not really cared for the name, but wanted to honor my father, Elmer Raymond Johnson.

One of my adolescent classmates in medical school used to torment me by calling me Esmeralda, the prostitute from the *Hunchback of Notre Dame*. Many of my classmates were crude, and it seemed the richer the family background, the cruder the behavior.

After living in Savannah for five years, Mother and I moved back to the farm. The next three years proved to be pleasant enough with no major upheavals in our lives until Mama Parker's death. She developed Hodgkin's lymphoma a few years before she died at the age of 72. The doctors operated on her neck and she was given radiation treatments; the worse part is that the surgeon cut part of the facial nerve that controlled the muscles in her lip and she had a distorted mouth thereafter. Mama Parker was a proud woman, so this was a tremendous blow for her. Furthermore, she developed terrible boils because of the depressed immunity that the cancer and the radiation treatments caused. I was not prepared for her death and I made all sorts of bargains with God to let her live. She was the fabric that held us together.

Mama Parker cooked many delicious dishes for the family throughout her life with us. She loved to spoil me and I was rewarded with afternoon treats; my favorite was rice pudding with raisins, flavored with lemons. It was luscious! She was a great homemaker and when she died, the whole rhythm of the farm died with her. The gardens went fallow, the house lost its loving care and nothing was really ever the same. Several months before she died, as if to try to fill the coming void, my parents adopted a baby from the community. I remember her telling my mother, "I helped you raise Joan, I am in no shape to help you now; you're on your own." There should have been more discussion about the adoption, but I was not party to it. One day the baby boy just came into our lives, courtesy of my mother.

John Wesley was the third child born to a family that just didn't think they could take care of him; he was six months old and only weighted 15 pounds. I was 17 years old, getting ready to leave for college, so escaped having to change many diapers along with other childcare responsibilities. Johnny was a cute blond haired, blue-eyed baby when he came to live with us. It was easy to become attached to such a beautiful little boy. At the time of the adoption my mother was 48 and my dad was 50. My Uncle Earl was extremely upset about the adoption because he knew they were saddling themselves with far too many duties for their stage in life. My father had never been actively involved in child rearing, so this responsibility would fall to my mother.

During my high school years and before Johnny's adoption, I drew closer to my dad. I understood more about his work and had a sense of pride in seeing him at the pecan auctions buying up his next year's supply for the shelled nut business. Perhaps he seemed more powerful and in control of things to me at those times than he did at home. My mother seldom had any praise for him.

I often helped Dad pack the one lb. bags of shelled pecans after school. By the mid '50s, he had a lot invested in equipment. Because he was shelling and packing large quantities of pecans the machinery often ran night and day during the busiest season, just before Thanksgiving. He had hired several of the local women to pick out pieces of the shell as the nuts ran through on a conveyor belt. The process was complicated and the pecan traveled through three or four machines before the shelled pecan was ready for packaging. Initially the nuts were fed through a specially designed mechanical device with measured rotating slots for each pecan to be gently smashed by a piston. The cracked nuts then fell into a large metal container for further mechanical handling along with blowers that helped remove the light loose shells and eventually went to conveyor belts, where the women worked. My dad gave employment to many people in the community, including me. I was not only efficient, but also fast and often packed 200 pounds of shelled nuts in an afternoon. The best part of packing was eating an occasional pecan. I loved pecans! Still do.

In the early days of my father's business, he rented space and equipment. As his profits grew, he moved his business to the country store and expanded the store over the years to a total of 2400 sq feet——it became the E.R. Johnson Shelled Pecans Company and since our house sat at an angle behind the store, my mother often remarked, "Raymond will not be happy until that store is in our front yard."

The country store, which had done well in the early '50s, was in decline by the '60s. There had always been several stores in the area because it was the intersection of two highways. Mr. Holsworth, my great grandfather, had operated a similar store at the beginning of the 20th century and my mother, Beatrice, had grown up in sales. I think this is where my mother met my dad. At one time, she had a candy route. I'm not sure if she sold candy along the way when she did her adult literacy program, but it was her way of making extra money by selling candy. Her grandfather had run a country store and she and my dad eventually opened their own in 1950.

Their country store had carried large crates of various kinds of fruits, such as raisins that were shipped loose; there was not much prepackaging. In the fifties the raisins, sausage, hot dogs, and wheels of cheese were weighed and sacked by the grocer. Later on, we sold gasoline, which was about 25 cents a gallon. With better transportation and the large freezers and refrigerators, which came along later, most country stores went out of business. My dad was fortunate that he had slowly expanded his business.

My dad's work was dusty, so his hands were dry and scaly, often even cracked open. The nearest dermatologist was 75 miles away and he was of little real help. Dad often got advice from salesmen who came from the big city, traveled around, and talked to a lot of people. One of them recommended Corn Husker's lotion; it was a good suggestion. Although it did not cure his problem, it certainly helped. My grandmother also got a good tip from a drummer (a common Southern term for salesman) when she complained of sore thumbs (paronychia). He told her she needed to get gloves for a lot of her wet work and it all but cured her problem. My dad probably had a form of hand and foot psoriasis, in medical jargon, Palmar/Plantar Psoriasis. He also tried out bag balm, which was used for the udders of milk cows, finding it quite helpful.

The farther you got away from the Deep South, the more prosperous business looked. My dad, who was called Johnson by many people, was most fortunate when he found a congealed fruit salad and processed cheese spread business that used his pecans. This business was located in Johnson City, Tennessee, and we as a family went with him on more than one business occasion. Johnson City, his namesake, turned out to be a windfall for his business. However, I never did appreciate the long waits at the time when he would leave my mother and me in the car. I remember being so bored waiting for him. There weren't any shopping malls to visit then, so we had to wait as patiently as was possible. These trips to North Carolina and Tennessee gave us opportunity to explore the area. While I was in high school, my Mom and Dad bought a place on the North Carolina/Tennessee state line, called Sam's Gap. The name had a nice ring to it—Sam was his dad's first name.

I had always helped my dad, even as a youngster of only nine years old. After the pecans were sorted by size and weight, the large burlap bags had to be closed using twine and a large needle. This was my first exposure to his work. Later while I was still in high school, I operated the country store after school, pumping gas and selling snacks and soda pop. As mentioned before, my other duties included weighing the shelled pecans in one-pound bags and getting the orders ready for delivery. I did receive a small sum of money, but I don't remember exactly the amount.

I never felt afraid to be alone at the country store. My family had warned me about shady characters that might come around and emphasized, if I ever felt threatened to "high tail" it out the back door. This occasion did arise when the gasoline deliveryman got out of line. The details are vague, but I was uncomfortable and left the store quickly. My mother called and complained and I think that the deliveryman may have been fired. I learned to dodge more than one advance. I had grown up in a matriarchal group and my grandmother had instilled in me a distrust of men, which probably wasn't all bad. Today, psychologist might look at it differently. Years later, I learned my grandmother may have been raped and this had colored her perspective accordingly; she did not want to have a granddaughter who had not been forewarned.

Mama Parker had filled my head with enough sexual information to give a child plenty of room for fantasy. Looking back I can see she was lonely and frustrated and she prompted me to act out some of her frustrations. It was as if she was saying, "I'm alone and unhappy so how can I let others be happy together?" Once she prompted me to intrude on my Mother and Dad during their sexual intercourse. "Run in and throw back the covers, Joan, and ask them what they're doing." I did and found that they were both stark naked and wondered what they could be doing in Mama Parker's feather bed so early in the evening. That was a strange thing, but she did have the only feather bed in the house and it was winter.

On other occasions when Mom and Dad went off to their own room and I was sleeping with Mama Parker, she'd tell me, "They're fucking, Joan." Not knowing exactly what that meant, the disdain with which she said it, made me angry, so I slammed our bedroom door. She was disdainful because she hadn't had sex often enough to have learned to enjoy it. My grandmother was an ambivalent woman, but I loved her dearly. She was occasionally teased about getting another husband and one of her favorite sayings was "I wouldn't have him if he had gold balls!"

To Mama Parker a man was just out "to get what he could", and then he would leave for another "easy make". She certainly instilled the fear of God in me about sex, and I was suspicious of any fellow who made any overtures toward me until I was twenty-three. Later on, my Aunt Bertha told me the well-kept secret about my grandmother. She had entered marriage carrying another man's child. The knowledge of this situation helped me to understand why Mama Parker felt the way she did. Who knows, she was at least jilted or raped at the very worst.

Everyone joked about my Grandpa Johnson, my dad's father, making overtures toward my grandmother Parker. He had been a widower for 15 or 20 years and was a frequent visitor at the farm for some years until she gave him a piece of her mind. They were always arguing over one thing or another about religion. Grandpa Johnson was a "hard shell" Baptist and my grandmother was a second generation Mormon. The main point of contention as I recall, was the Mormons' refusal to preach the Grace of Jesus Christ. Grandpa Sam, as we called him, considered himself a sinner and often hummed *Amazing Grace* and praised his Lord

Jesus for saving him. I grew up disliking that song, since it made us seem like hopeless sinners. Now when I hear it, I reflect on their arguments and think he was right after all. I have come to love *Amazing Grace*.

My grandmother's youngest sister, Melba lived within a few miles of the farm. She was 11 years younger and attached to my grandmother. They often played cards in the afternoon and it was pleasant when she came and spent time at our house. These sisters were both toothless, older ladies, who could not wear their dentures. They often spoke nostalgically about their own pretty teeth. At one time many doctors recommended tooth extractions to cure many ailments, especially rheumatism or other inflammatory diseases, neither one of them had such an affliction; however, they were probably not predisposed either. My great aunt had a weakness for whiskey and sometimes drank too much. Regrettably, this carried over to her only son Danny who became an alcoholic. However, as I was growing up I thought the world of Danny and his wife Vivian—my movie buddies.

Few people like to travel alone and my dad was no exception. Grandpa Sam, his father, used to travel with him on his pecan route. Several uncles, friends and eventually I made some trips with him. He especially enjoyed telling some of his customers about my being admitted to medical school, even though he often said, "Getting a medical license is just having a license to steal." He thought people were always at the mercy of the medical system when they got sick. You couldn't shop around. Knowledge is power and the doctors had all the power in those days. There was no Google or Wikipedia.

Although I am a physician today, I think there is quite a bit of truth in what he thought and said about the medical system. Doctors often find it hard to make decisions about personal or family health in a capitalistic health system. However, today the medical system has become even more complex with big pharmaceutical companies, huge insurance companies, and so called non-profit hospital systems. The doctors are only part of the tangled web called healthcare.

My dad often did not buy a radio for his truck. If he did, we seldom played it. Anyway, the radio reception when you traveled wasn't that good. He loved to sing and yodel. This was true of his whole family I learned later. Sometimes I would sing with him but there were many songs like the *Wabash Cannon Ball* that I had never heard. There were five verses and he knew most of them:

> *From the great Atlantic Ocean,*
> *To the wide Pacific shore.*
> *From the green of blooming mountains*
> *To the ivy by the door.*
> *She's a mighty tall and handsome*
> *And quite well-known by all.*
> *She's the modern combination—*
> *Chorus--On the Wabash Cannon Ball*
> *She came down from Birmingham*
> *One cold December day*
> *As she rolled into the station.*
> *You could hear the people say,*
> *There's a girl from Tennessee,*
> *She's long and she is tall,*
> *She came down from Memphis—*
> *Chorus—On the Wabash Cannon Ball*

This song about a locomotive and travel was appropriate for him.

When I was on break from college or medical school I often rode along with my dad for company. My study routine was vigorous: I never took time off from school. Still there were a few weeks break to be enjoyed, and so these trips with him gave us a chance to spend some time together. We got a little cabin when Mother and Johnny came along. Mother was not much for roughing it or camping. My little brother was only three or four at this time and was beginning to be a lot of responsibility for her. An "on the road dad" did not help matters, but he made good money and probably was home as much as many other dads.

My dad had a self-deprecating sense of humor and was entertaining. He sang, *You Are My Sunshine* a lot. At the time, it was just a song and I didn't think he was singing about me, but I realize now that maybe he was. He sang other western type songs like "Home on the Range" and "She'll Be Coming 'Round the Mountain." He loved to yodel like some of the country singers of the '50s such as Eddie Arnold and because he was so amiable, and a good listener, many people liked his company.

Dad loved the North Carolina/Tennessee Mountains, probably more than my mother. So, he was pleased when the land at Sam's Gap, Tennessee, became available. He had come to know his business route fairly well over the years and made friends with an Appalachian family by the name of McCann, who lived just up the road from Sam's Gap. The McCann family's home sat above an artesian well, where everyone stopped for the cold, fresh water coming out of the mountain.

In the late '60s the McCanns still used an outhouse. They had a least two blind children out of four; I found out later, it was a congenital blindness. One son still lived at home, but the older son lived in Asheville and visited his family often. A.J., as he was called, worked at the blind school and was quite articulate. It was the first time I had ever had my face "read" by a blind person. He took his hands and gently went over my face. They had two married daughters who were not blind and had moved away from the area. I think the McCanns were happy to have some neighbors, even though my father was only there for a few weeks at a time and not more than three or four times a year.

My dad and Mr. McCann were good friends. In fact, I am almost certain that he gave an unsecured loan of $5000 to buy the property at Sam's Gap. It was a trust that did not disappoint and my father repaid the loan within a few years. The cool air of the mountains was so refreshing in the summer; a place to escape the oppressive heat in Georgia.

There was a little house on the property. It was really more of a shack, but my Dad fixed it up. He ran water using flexible tubing from a spring that was located back of the house on the mountainside and created a storage tank for it. He also installed a toilet and I was turned loose with a can of paint and paintbrush. It was slightly better than camping.

Mr. McCann loved to talk about the big house down in Asheville that the Vanderbilts had built. It would be several decades before I visited the Biltmore Castle with my husband and children. George Vanderbilt bought 8000 acres and had all kinds of enterprises going at one time. A man with unlimited funds, before income taxes, could do a lot for such a poor area. He built a 250-room chateau which was finished in 1895. Mr. McCann's description of it did not disappoint; it was, however, a great contrast to how most people in the area lived.

It is so important to have the capacity to give, as well as to receive love. If a family or friends received a gift of fruit or vegetables from my dad, it was always the best according to our neighbors. They spoke fondly of him, even many years after his death and commented on how generous he had been with them. I did not know this side of him growing up. He could be stingy; sometimes it was to his and our family's detriment.

In my twenties, I began to appreciate my dad's side of the family. My family found an old photo of my paternal grandmother and grandfather pictured with their first two children that needed some restoration. Taking the task on, I went so far as to have the work done with a small deposit. The restored photograph was beautiful but costly; my dad refused to come up with the final payment of $100. I sadly had to return it to the store.

Another disappointment came on the day of my graduation from medical school. I thought it would be nice to go to the Holiday Inn for lunch to celebrate this milestone in my life. My dad and I were riding with my Uncle Earl and Aunt Bertha. After suggesting lunch at the hotel's restaurant, he bolted out of the car when we stopped for a red light. We were all flabbergasted. He gave us no reason for this behavior and became a "screaming banshee." This was an example of poor anger management. Later it became apparent to me that he had an aversion for "corporate chains," be it food or hotels. He probably saw it as a threat to the small business owner; however, he had no way of expressing what was bothering him. I had seen him explode over little things in the past, most of the incidents stemmed around money.

No one knew what was going on in his mind, perhaps not even my dad. We wound up eating at a diner down the road, even though he could have afforded to pay for lunch for six at the Holiday Inn. He just did not have any graciousness in him on one of the most important days of my life. On the other hand, if he had had a credit card, he might have been gracious and worried about the money later. I don't know why someone, including me, did not think about a meal of celebration. No one had made a plan.

My uncle and aunt also had money and could have stepped up, but they didn't. It was somewhat of a tarnished day for me. How could I complain when he had made all those tuition payments, leaving me debt free, when I finished medical school? That was a big thing, but as the saying goes, "It's the little things that count." It was a disappointment I never forgot. I felt I just wasn't worth it! It should have been a celebration for our whole family.

In 1969 after I had finished my internship in Utah, he helped drive me to Philadelphia and was fascinated that I had a credit card and paid for all our expenses. The times were changing. Someone once said, "Your children push you into the future"—somehow this did not happen with my family.

Without memory, there is no healing.
Without forgiveness, there is no future.

                                      Archbishop Desmond Tutu

Chapter Seven
Family Struggles

I was looking for peace and harmony in my family, but it kept eluding us; it made me such a sad soul. Our lives seemed to center around coping with my mother's illness and strange behavior. Her bouts with bulimia and depression continued off and on for years. As a child and even all through my time in medical school, I was unaware of the fact that she had bulimia. It is only with my knowledge of medicine that can now look back with a better understanding of her illness. She would get a "sick headache" and then forced herself to vomit. Subsequently, she developed osteoporosis, which is a side effect of bulimia. Coca Cola was her favorite beverage. Heavy consumption of these carbonated beverages also increased her risk for osteoporosis. Cola beverages contain phosphorous in the form of phosphoric acid, which can interfere with the absorption of calcium. In 1966, Mother received a medical disability due to her overall weakened physical shape.

Her family doctor recommended to my father and me that she should be seen by a psychiatrist. I proceeded to make arrangements at the medical college. His assessment was that she had ambivalent feelings toward my grandmother Mama Parker, which she could not resolve. Mama Parker had been gone five years and she felt more and more isolated with feelings of hopelessness. In addition, my parents were not the closest any more. The psychiatrist also hinted that her most successful years were in Savannah, when she had been away from my father and that there were continual issues in their marriage. Mother was menopausal, so she was given some hormones along with an antidepressant to help snap her out of her depression. The hormones caused her to bleed producing another subset of problems. She seemed to rally, so by the time I graduated from medical school, she, my little brother and my dad traveled with me to my internship in Salt Lake City, Utah.

Actually, there had not been that much to move. Books were the bane of my existence as a student. Room and board were included in my work agreement, so I was given a sparely furnished apartment close to the hospital. My mom helped me buy a few items for the kitchen, and this change of pace was a pleasant experience for both of us. Happily, looking forward to my own apartment, I even rented a piano for the year! Music had always been a great escape for me. Playing the piano gave me a place in the world where I could vent my joys and disappointments.

My mother had pushed me into an untenable life; she had brought me up Mormon, pushed me through the temple and now at the age of 24, I wanted to find someone with whom to share my life. My family seemed supportive at the time, but in retrospect, this may have been more harmful than good. I did not want to struggle all through my life with religion like my mother. There was so much ambivalence about religion in our family between the Baptist and the Mormons.

{Archived letters are being used to help establish the frame of mind of the writers. Reading these decades later has provided useful information that I had not observed earlier. Now, I realize how scattered my mother's thoughts had become.}

After I was settled in Salt Lake City, in late summer of 1968, I received a letter from Mother. She often did not date her letters. It simply read "Saturday PM".

Dearest Joan,

I received the cards Thursday and Johnny thinks they are so pretty. Cindy (a neighbor's granddaughter) asked for him to go down at her Grandpa's to play, so that is where he is. Friday I received your letter and Tuesday I got the antibiotics. It sure did look lonesome without you in Augusta [where I finished Medical School].

They are having my brace sent by Air Mail and plan to call me when it arrives. [She suffered with several collapsed vertebrae because of osteoporosis]

I'm sending you the best news I can send. If things work out money wise Johnny and I will spend Christmas with you, if I can wait that long. I drove to Augusta and back Tuesday; it got the best of me. I stayed in bed just about all day Wednesday. [This remark about her and Johnny's coming out for Christmas surprised me. What about Dad? She had never flown in an airplane, so her remark puzzled me.]

Your dad will come back tomorrow or Monday. He takes his pistol and a new 12-gauge shotgun with him. He sure is brave. Raymond has been up to Johnson City, Tennessee delivering a load of shelled pecans.

We have so many nice butternut squash and if I can find a basket I'll send you and Zina some of them. The new Irish Potatoes are good too. We have okra but I cannot stand to cut that fuzzy stuff. It may be too hard when Raymond gets back.

Be sure and send my letter back from Dr. Pittman. It is hot here, but I make out OK with the fan and air conditioner. Your dad has found out that my room is the best room for him to sleep in. I cannot stand heat. Johnny will call him at night and say "Daddy, you know what the book tells you to do. . ."

Last night Johnny said, "Mother, when you die—this is the best place in the world." He is so good when my head aches—he would walk any distance for me to get well. He will kiss me and rub my head and back. Johnny is so sweet.

Evelyn is in Florida. Mr. and Mrs. Kent are in Chicago and Ellie Mae in Michigan visiting Rosalyn. She flew up there. Your dad is better and I was glad that Zina had your Grandpa Parker get his brace.

Joan, don't take chances in walking or driving. I'm glad you never get in a hurry. I was always on the fast side.

I may send this Monday. I'm nervous and I know you have a hard time reading this.

Guess my kidneys are some better but Dr. Ball knows very little, he gave me Gantrisin and never tested my urine. He is on the board for worn out

At the Crossroads: A Southern Daughter's Story

teachers and I'm not going to tell him what to do. Raymond said, "He just can not stand a 'good for nothing' like Ball." Dr. Ball thinks you and I love him beyond words.

Be sweet and write when you have time. I know it is hot where you are. I'm so cool and it is 98 degrees outside; a cool 70 in the den. You know me—stay cool.

Love, Mother

When I discussed my plans for the future, I told my family that I would take on a residency in a subspecialty of medicine such as dermatology, to narrow my field of general medicine to something that I could master. The stethoscopes of my era were not the quality of today, and listening to the heart sounds mortified me. Being a more visual person, general medicine was not a good fit, so I told my parents it would be more fulfilling to be a consultant, maybe a diagnostician in a more limited field of study.

During my third year of medical school, I had taken an elective in dermatology and saw its potential; therefore, in my senior year, it became my task to apply to various dermatology programs. I applied for a residency in Dermatology at the University of Pennsylvania, as well as Geisinger Institute, and the University of North Carolina. I was eventually accepted at all three places, but University of Pennsylvania was the first to send me an acceptance letter in the middle of September 1968, requiring a reply within two weeks. It was by far the most prestigious of the three, and I had to act right away; therefore I accepted the three year program which would start July 1, 1969, at Pennsylvania Hospital for a six-month rotation. I went on to work at three other hospitals in Philadelphia: the Hospital of the University of Pennsylvania, Graduate Hospital, Philadelphia General

Hospital, as well as Philadelphia's sexually transmitted disease clinic.

I met Benton between my junior and senior year of medical school. The Latter Day Saints Hospital offered students, who were starting their senior year, a summer semester of practicum. Each student was assigned to an intern. It was a friendly atmosphere and I met many nice people. I shared a house with a nurse and a medical student from England named Daphne. We all had some family connections in Utah that probably gave our own families a measure of comfort. Daphne had an aunt living in Salt Lake City and I had Grandpa Parker and his wife Zina. We did not have a car, so we counted on shared rides to cookouts and other planned events.

The following year when I returned to Salt Lake City to start my internship, Benton was getting ready to leave for Philadelphia for an ophthalmology program at Wills Eye Institute. I was disappointed he was leaving. Before he left, my acceptance letter from the University of Pennsylvania arrived, so he was one of the first persons I told about my good fortune. We hugged and congratulated one another and I said, "Well, I will probably be seeing you in Philadelphia." We had a comfortable relationship and my fondness for him had grown over time. I was attracted to him!

Benton had done his internship at Latter Day Saints Hospital before he went to Viet Nam. When he was finished with his tour of duty, he was happy to return to his old hospital to start a surgical residency. The surrounding mountains were an outlet for his hiking and rock climbing, and during the winter he had opportunities for skiing. My first impressions of Benton were positive. He was well spoken, was 30 years old, with a receding hairline, of medium build, standing about 5' 10", fair skinned with sandy blond hair and blue eyes. Benton was always enthusiastic about anything the group of interns and residents were doing, offering help to organize an overnight camping trek into the Uinta Mountains and Wasatch National Forest above Salt Lake. It was the first time I had slept in a tent in the wilderness. Great fun! Although he was not a Mormon, he appreciated the values they had and he was a clean living kind of guy who did not smoke or drink much. We all became good friends and enjoyed each other's company.

He had worked with the Forest Service in his summers off from college. Since his parents worked overseas, he had no home in the USA and most of his family's best friends lived back East. This work gave him room and board plus fresh air. He loved the out of doors. The work consisted of repairing trails and cutting brush to prevent forest fires. His group had to ride horse back to get to some of the remote areas. During those summers he had a lot of old cowboys as companions.

Benton had been with the Special Forces, better known as the Green Berets in Viet Nam in 1966. Even though Viet Nam was a war zone, he waxed enthusiastically about helping the undeveloped world. He had been stationed in Pleiku, which was located in the Central Highlands of South Viet Nam. His work had been with the Montagnards (French for mountaineers), as well as in the lowlands of Viet Nam. Benton was also a paratrooper. He never shunned a challenge and became certified in this field. He wanted to have access to remote areas where he could do the most good, even if he had to jump out of a plane.

The main function of his unit was to work with the indigenous population to not only train them to fight and defend themselves but also to teach them basic health practices in a community setting. Naturally, his first duty was to take care of the sick and wounded soldiers, as well as any villagers who wandered into his camp. Benton had treated many venomous snake bites that were often fatal, especially to young children. He taught rudimentary medicine to Vietnamese medics. After they had finished the basic course, he also had an advanced course that included such things as pulling teeth, suturing, and even treating cerebral malaria. These medics were treasured in the community. Benton upheld the motto of the Green Berets: De Opresso Liber— Free the oppressed.

Malaria was the most prevalent parasitic infection among the Vietnamese. The Walter Reed Army Research team stationed there discovered that fully 59% of the Montagnards carried the disease, suffering bouts of chills and fever whenever they were under stress, such as patrols with close contact to the Viet Cong. After two to three days, the crisis would be over from the malaria, and they were strong again.

He described the countryside of Viet Nam as he flew to remote areas in a Huey Helicopter. Benton noted the view from the air had been breathtakingly beautiful with the green dense jungles stretching all the way to the white sand beaches and the aqua-blue waters of the South China Sea. There were also vast expanses of grassland extending toward the mountains in the distance. In spite of being in a war zone, his conversations about his tour of duty seemed to satisfy his need for adventure.

Benton was excited about his residency at the prestigious Wills Eye Hospital and Research Institute in the late summer of 1968. When I arrived in July 1969, he had already had a year of surgery in addition to his extensive experience from being in Viet Nam. He also was fairly well situated with his living quarters.

Wills Eye was doing early research in cataract removal and lens implantation. This would be a new frontier in ophthalmology, one that eventually made many ophthalmologists millionaires within a few years. With the lens implantation procedure, people with cataracts who were practically blind no longer had to wear "coke bottle" glasses to see. It was the miracle of modern medicine. Most of the ophthalmologists earned at least $2000 per procedure, and they averaged 20 people on a scheduled OR (operating room) day. It was thought to be most risky, but after decades the payment to the doctors fell to $650 but not before eye clinic empires were built overnight.

I am not sure when my parents shifted their hopes and dreams to my life and career as their own dream. Initially, there was not much response from them about my acceptance in the dermatology program in Pennsylvania, and as the time drew near to begin my program, there was still no encouragement from home even though they knew it was what I had been longing to study. As long as I was in Georgia, or even later in Utah, they had some control, but my going to the Northeast would change all of our lives forever.

Correspondence continued and I did my best to call and write from my end. Long distance was still expensive, and as an intern with limited funds, we had short conversations regularly. I tried to write every week, and occasionally, received a short letter from my mother with some money tucked inside. This act of kindness was especially appreciated prior to my vacation to Hawaii.

After spending the Christmas of 1967 in Georgia with the psychiatrist and my mother, I needed a break from studies when my one-week vacation came around in December of 1968. The travel agency offered many appealing Hawaiian tours. If I went to Georgia for my week of vacation, I would lose 2 days traveling there and back and there might be four good days with the family. Being the dutiful daughter, gifts were bought and sent for everyone—mailed well before Christmas. In retrospect, my life might have turned out quite differently with a trip home. I was simply exhausted and deserved a carefree rest because I was definitely at my breaking point.

Like so many young people, I had imagined myself going to Hawaii since my teenage years. I had even received information from the University of Hawaii while in high school; geography was a favorite subject with dreams of travel someday. Utah was much closer to the Hawaiian Islands, making it possible for this dream to come true. I found an all-inclusive tour and decided to take it. Many of my colleagues had been there and encouraged me with some of their experiences. One of the nurses had a brother who lived there, and we had a pleasant date during my trip. He was really nice, a Mormon cowboy from Wyoming who longed to go back to the ranch.

Hawaii turned out to be everything I had envisioned it to be. Three islands were on my tour: Hawaii, the big island, with its volcano and the Kona coast where coffee is grown; then Oahu, where Honolulu and Diamond Head are located; and Maui, one of the smaller islands. The Mormon Church has a big Polynesian cultural center with a temple on Oahu, where they offered an afternoon and evening tour including dinner—that was most enjoyable. There was also a day trip to Maui, an old whaling port, where I had a picnic lunch on the wharf. Although alone, it was one of the best vacations ever experienced. It was fun buying souvenirs for everyone in my family and I looked forward to sharing my experiences with them.

At the beginning of December, I received a letter from Benton. He planned to be in Salt Lake City over New Year's:

> *I wonder if you will be back from the land of "Aloha" by then. Of course, the main item on the agenda will be skiing and reunions with everybody and I'm sure the hospital may have a few charts for me to sign. If you are too busy maybe we can get together over a cup of hot chocolate and discuss the coming year.*
>
> *Ophthalmology is going well and I'm learning the ropes slowly but surely. Philadelphia, I can*

> now tolerate and am beginning to enjoy some of its advantages. It has turned cold here but still no snow. I sure am looking forward to that dry Utah powder snow.
>
> Have a good time in Hawaii but watch out for all those service men on R&R from Viet Nam.

As Ever,
Benton

Over New Year's we had a wonderful first date, and I felt that romance was in the air as he kissed me softly on the lips at the end of the lovely evening we spent together. He was a real gentleman. He was so kind and I really enjoyed his sense of humor. We simply relished each other's company. I felt we had a good chance to build it into something more. He promised to help me locate an apartment in Philadelphia when my Dad and I arrived the following summer.

Letters from home and phone calls continued:

December 1968
Dearest Joan,

> *I have squeezed some money out of your dad and Johnny is sending you $5.00. He had a bad case of measles. If he is better tomorrow, I hope I can send him to school on Friday [Johnny was seven]. He is thrilled over his birthday tomorrow. I will try and make pictures and you will have them when you get back from Hawaii.*
>
> *Sure hope your throat is better. Your dad went to Johnson City, Tennessee, this morning. As usual he left around 4 A.M. I sure hope he makes it over the ice and snow. He laughs and will say, "I'm glad Joan is enjoying the ice and snow out in Utah."*

Adding further, "Nobody can tell her nothing, she knows it all." I told him you were OK.

Love, Mother

Friday AM, January 3, 1969
"Dearest Joan,

It sure did take a load off my heart to know that you were back in SLC. I sat up all night Christmas night and Dec 26th. Ray said, "Did Joan call? I said," No," but when the mail came we got the address where you were staying and he wanted me to call.

I do not have any trouble having Johnny and Ray brushing their teeth. (I had sent them electric toothbrushes.) We enjoy the toothbrushes. Everything is so nice that you sent us for Christmas.

Donna the colored woman was cleaning up the kitchen. I took 10 of my headache caps out of the bottle and put the others on the shelf. We were throwing away old bottles, papers and other things and she threw them in the trash. I carried three boxes to the litter barrel. Afterwards it poured down rain and I knew the headache medicine was gone. That's my luck!"

I am taking calcium lactate for my bones. My head aches all the time.

Johnny has a 5-speed bike, racer car, two crows on a fence that he can shoot at with his pop gun. He sure is happy. He missed 5 days of school with the measles. He only had fever for one day and got along fine.

At the Crossroads: A Southern Daughter's Story

Your dad doesn't think you should spend money coming home in March, when we will be in Salt Lake City in June.

Since Christmas, every day seems like Sunday. You meet people in town and they say,

"What day is it? Monday or Friday?" Ray asked me to enclose a penny from him.

Love, Mother

{From birth I had on occasions been called either "Baby Boy" supposedly because I had no hair, later this became "Baby Girl". This is a uniquely Southern custom.}

February 6, 1969 Wednesday

Dearest Baby Girl,
I received your letter and I'm sorry about you having trouble with your teeth. I have my car paid for, and a new set of tires paid for, plan to have them put on in May. [I was having my wisdom teeth extracted at a dentist's office—which turned out to be the most painful procedure I had ever experienced. He did it under local anesthesia and I think each tooth extraction cost $25.00!]

I will send you some extra money soon—are you paying tithing?

Ray got his package from you today, it was torn terribly. Thought I'd let him finish opening it when he gets in Thursday or Friday. [I was late in getting his birthday gift in the mail].

My back is killing me. It's the bones not the muscles. Don't let it cross your mind.

I bought myself three new dresses yesterday. Johnny got some new dress slippers. He is going to give a 2 ½ minute talk at Sunday school soon. Clark Hankins from the Mormon Church went to Salt Lake City, I don't know if you saw him.

I had lunch in Dublin—everyone I met had to tell me how good I looked. I'll eat in Vidalia today. I have a new color TV and I have a booster on the antenna that will let me play the old one in my room. It is where it always sat when Mama was living.

Yesterday I took Johnny to school and his teacher Mrs. Powell will be getting married in May. She asked me to sit with her family so that I could be her Mama. You know Tim Ward married her sister and James Hormel also married another one. I forgot to mention that Jim will get his PhD in history from GA Southern this summer. He is teaching there also. I do wish I lived where Johnny could have music and dancing. The nearest place is Dublin and it isn't the best.

I have some new curtains in the den. Ray put them up.

It's time to get Johnny up, his cartoon club will be on soon and then to Mr. Davis for him to catch the bus.

Be sweet and write. Love, Mother

Another letter came during the late winter of 1968-69 from my dad. He must have sent a cartoon clipping from the paper.

At the Crossroads: A Southern Daughter's Story

Dear Baby,

This reminds me of when I let you and Junior Wynn's boy go with me to the Atlanta Farmer market with a load of peas, melons, onions and other stuff. He wet the quilt and said, "It must have rained last night." You remember we gave out of gas on the edge of the city and I had to go and get some to go on. We had a good time. Wish we could go back over it all. I love you, Daddy. P.S. I've been in the house two days reading the paper and other things.

Although there were some problems at home, the situation sounded under a lot better control than it had the previous year. So I was relieved to get their letters. We continued to write. My internship was demanding, but not overwhelming. Nonetheless, I was tired and glad to be finishing up.

My family was coming out in June to help me move to Philadelphia. In April, I got another letter from my father.

April 14, 1969
Joan,

I have been up to Johnson City, Tennessee for a weekend and stopped at Sam's Gap, spent the night. I have been thinking about you and you going to Pennsylvania. It is a nigger city, a bad place for white folks to stay. Everybody I talk to says, "Hell you are not going there are you!" I tell them no; I wonder how far it is from here. If I were you I would not go there. Why don't you come somewhere around here and practice for a year and then make up your mind what you want to be. I had a good offer to sell Sam's Gap. We are not getting no younger. Your, Paw

I tried to explain that this was the brass ring and I needed to grab it. Residency positions like this did not come along every day. In retrospect, they had little understanding about what was at stake for me. I did not like practicing general medicine and the times were changing. No longer could a doctor just finish an internship and immediately hang out a shingle. My parents had their own fantastic goals for me, but they never considered what I wanted to be and what my visions were. My dad had flown along with a friend of his and me from Atlanta to NYC in the early 60's to see about expanding his business, so saying he didn't know how far Philadelphia would be from home was playing dumb.

Late in the spring I wrote home saying that I really wanted to take the residency program in Philadelphia. It was a wonderful opportunity.

On May 12, 1969, after I sent her flowers for Mother's day, I received this letter from my mother.

> *Dearest Joan,*
>
> *Only a few lines to let you know on Saturday evening, Arthur delivered the roses. She used local flowers and they had all but died overnight. I have some in the yard that could "put hers in the shade." [meaning the flowers were inferior]*
>
> *Ray went with us to Sunday school yesterday and Johnny said, "Dad are you going to let Grandpa Parker baptize you?" He said, "I don't know."*
>
> *Joan, send my mail to my post office address. Every letter you send has been opened and most of Ray's too.*
>
> *I'm here in Vidalia having new tires put on the car for the trip out West. Ellie Mae is coming*

At the Crossroads: A Southern Daughter's Story

Thursday at 9 AM to clean the house. She will go back on the following Wednesday.

I am looking forward to seeing her.

We are having new potatoes, radishes, mustard and onions out of the garden. I'm doing all I can to keep things going, but it takes a lot out of you.
Be sweet and kind
Give my love to all,
Mother

Shortly before they came to Salt Lake City, I wrote my Mom a quick letter.

Dearest Mother,
I'm sorry I haven't written you a nice long letter in a while—will try and fill up every available space on this page. It was good to hear your voice this morning and I appreciate your sweet letters. Also the pair of panty hose you sent.

I'm off the Medicine wards for a month and am taking an elective in infectious diseases with one of the professors from the University of Utah. I will have no night call so this will be nice. On Call at the hospital is getting pretty old by now and I'm looking forward to a residency in dermatology which has essentially no night call. Being an intern means hard work, not enough sleep and stress.

I had Sunday dinner with the folks (Grandpa Parker and Zina)—they always want to know when I've heard from you. Will try and remember to send you their phone numbers at the end of this letter. I'm sorry I haven't done it yet.

> *Aunt Vickie (she was Grandpa Parker's sister) has recovered from her operation just fine. She lives by herself and I'm sure she is lonesome. While I was down at the folks, she called up and talked to Zina a long time (30 to 40 minutes).*
>
> *Do you need any more medicine for headaches such as Fiorinal?*
>
> *I'm not in much of a writing mood. My period started today and my back is killing me. Also have a splitting headache.*
>
> *The folks want to know definitely if you will go with them up to Lava Hot Springs for a few days when you arrive. I told them I thought you would but make up your mind definitely. Phone numbers: area code 801 and numbers given for Grandpa and Zina as well as Lewis and his wife.*
>
> *Take care of yourself,*
> *Love always, Joan*

My mother also tried to coach my brother into writing, so in the spring I got a letter from him too. Mama Parker had always been called Sis or Sissy by her siblings and relatives, so my mother encouraged my brother Johnny to call me Sissy.

> *Dearest Sissy,*
> *I love you and Mother tells me you love me too. Sissy, I am the only brother you have.*
>
> *Just think, Sissy, I can play Jingle Bells with both hands; you are going to feel proud of me some day.*
>
> *I'm sending you my old math paper to show you how good I am.*

At the Crossroads: A Southern Daughter's Story

I love the church, and Sunday school.
If you have time write me.
Your brother, Johnny

I really didn't like being manipulated or the passive aggressive tones that were developing between my parents and me. They often reminded me that if something happened to them, I would be responsible for Johnny. They didn't seem to be able to discuss anything openly or see my point of view. During my senior year of medical school, I went to the bank where my father often secured loans for his business and asked for a loan on my car. My parents had a fit! My mom and dad said, "Why would you think you had to borrow money from the bank?"

I felt I was a financial burden for them. My mother was manifesting more emotional problems, which brought on more of her "sick headaches." There was a singular patient with this disorder in my psychiatric rotation at the medical college, and the root of the problem often came from the patient's feelings that they had no control over his/her own life and no influence in the lives of others.

The winter before my graduating from medical school, my mother was in a horrible mental state of mind. My father was off traveling and not available. Even though there had been some hostile encounters with mother, the climax came when she grabbed a pair of scissors, and came at me with them. A shocking experience! Knowing that she would need more psychiatric treatment, I thought borrowing some money for my last year of medical school, would help out. I eventually paid off the loan, but my parents and I were in a power struggle and it was not about financing my education. They did not want me to be independent of them; they wanted absolute control of my life.

Anyway, when I was finished my internship in June, Mother, Johnny, and my dad all came out to Salt Lake City. To everyone's surprise my dad was baptized into the Mormon faith at the Tabernacle on Temple Square by Grandpa Parker. The Parkers were well pleased that they had succeeded because my dad had been a hard shell to crack. My dad was now a bona fide Mormon.

I was really quite surprised, but my mother had been working on him through my little brother. It was a momentous occasion; Dad was 58 years old. Mormons are always looking for souls and he probably thought this would improve our family. My mother seemed well and happy about it. Although still a Mormon, some reservations entered my mind. More and more it seemed a bit too patriarchal for me, and women seemed to be treated as second-class members, always submissive to the men. I had ambivalent feelings now about my dad's conversion. Like most religions, Mormonism riddles its members, intentionally or unintentionally, with guilt.

My father helped me drive to Philadelphia. I had contacts with a Mormon girl who had moved there, and she was kind enough to offer me her sofa for a few days while searching for an apartment. Finding a place in the big city was an overwhelming experience for me.

My dad met Benton and we had a meal together. Dad and I had stayed at a motel on the outskirts of Philadelphia, where Benton came to meet us. By all outward appearances everyone hit it off well; my dad was pleasant, hospitable, and paid for the meal.

It had been planned that someone from the family in Salt Lake City would help drive my mom and brother back to the farm. My dad would fly home from Philadelphia; however, our planning was not without some drama. When we called home to check on Mother and Johnny, Dad learned his garage, which housed a tractor and some other equipment, was on fire. The two-story building with an upstairs apartment was situated about 50 yards from the house. With no fire department nearby, it burned to the ground. No time for my dad to see a little of Philadelphia and get better acquainted with Benton.

I found a place to live in West Philadelphia. It was on Beaumont Street, not too far from the hospital. The area was riddled with crime, and before long, my car battery was stolen. Then an even scarier and tragic event happened; a girl in the neighborhood was raped. During my internship, in a weak moment, I had adopted a puppy, "Mr. Chips," who traveled with us to Philadelphia. He was a great comfort to me, but after the rape, I became fearful to take my little Scottish terrier out for his walks; fortunately, there was a backyard with the first floor apartment. My rent was half of my paycheck from the University, but somehow I managed to stay solvent even though there was barely a $5 or $10 balance in the checking account many months.

Benton often invited me to escape the city; taking trips to Lancaster, PA to the Amish country or hiking around Valley Forge or visiting one of the many museums that Philadelphia has to offer. We both enjoyed watercolors, so sometimes we sketched and painted when the weather was nice. Our friendship blossomed into a romance. He invited me to a dance given by his university that was held at a men's club that did not allow women to be members. My generation would be changing things, ever so slowly.

It was a wonderful courtship. One of the songs John Lennon and Paul McCartney wrote reminds me of those days. *"Someday when we're dreaming, deep in love, not a lot to say, then we will remember, things we said today."*

Benton and I often received tickets from professors when they had a conflict in their schedules and they knew we would appreciate a night on the town. We went to several musicals,

Jean Gotlieb Bradley

The Man from La Mancha, Fiddler on the Roof, Jesus Christ Superstar, and even an opera, *Cavalleria Rusticana*. This was my first opera and little did I realize, my life would some day mirror the same drama presented in this opera.

Where there is room in the heart there is always room in the house.

          Thomas Moore

Chapter Eight
Leaving Georgia

In December, I started thinking about Christmas vacation, but as a first-year resident I had little time off. It hardly seemed worth flying for two days to spend two days at home. A letter from my Uncle Bob, who was my father's youngest brother, arrived in the mail. He and I always had a good relationship. In fact he gave me the most money for my graduation from medical school. $200 was a lot of money!

In early December 1969, he wrote

> *Dearest Joan,*
> *Will answer your letter received last week. And was I glad to hear from you; it had been so long since I had heard from you. I am very well. Having some trouble with my elbow; guess I am getting too much sweetner [sic]. Hope you are fine.*
>
> *I went over to help your Daddy on Friday. Your Mother was gone, but she came in about 2 o'clock. Your Daddy is having trouble with his stomach that is for sure. It must be an ulcer for he bent doubled over several times and laid down on the floor. He*

At the Crossroads: A Southern Daughter's Story

ate 2 ham sandwiches and a piece of cake and it like to have killed him.

I told him to go to the hospital and have something done for it. He cries a lot about you but your Mother, it don't seem to bother her too much, but I might be wrong. She told him not to take that medicine you sent him. She told him it might run him crazy or something like that.

Well, honey I wish you could be close by. I might just switch doctors and go to a sweet, pretty one like you. I know you are better than anything we have in Lyons. I got an appointment on 12-16-69, so if you are coming I will just put it off. I love you more than any of my nieces.

Listen, I would like for you to see your Daddy just for a few minutes but don't come just because I want you to. I know it would help him a lot.

Johnny is a good little boy; he calls me Uncle Bobby and him and me really worked hard Friday. Don't tell any one about this letter. I read the one you sent to me and your Daddy cried. I did not tell your Mother about your letter so don't you either. Write soon as you can. I love you very much, Your Uncle Bob. [I don't recall exactly what I had written him, but it probably had to do with my family's not accepting Benton as my choice for a companion.]

My residency in dermatology was going well, and it felt like, at last, I had found my niche in medicine. After this letter from my Uncle Bob, and with some conversations with my father on the phone, I asked Benton if he would like to travel to the Smokey Mountains during a long holiday weekend. Loving and trusting my dad so much, it was my wish for him to get to know Benton better. His cabin was situated close to the Appalachian Trail and I knew Benton would enjoy the hikes around there. He was also interested in the McCann family and the familial blindness that had afflicted them.

My parents knew I was seeing Benton, and that he'd been invited to make the trip to visit Sam's Gap. Benton insisted that they should know he was going into the mission field. At the time, it seemed too early to burden them with this information; maybe, we should wait until they got to know him better. Praising his high moral values, I told them he was a good Christian who wanted to serve in the missionary field. His parents were in Nepal working at the United Mission; his dad was British and his mom was American. He had been born in India while they were working there. I reminded my dad that he had met Benton when we drove to Philadelphia.

We drove down to meet my dad at Sam's Gap and Dad had brought a cousin along with whom I was acquainted. We chatted for awhile, although his cousin didn't say very much. There was some rain in the weather forecast, and we wanted to take a hike on the trail while the weather was still good, so we told Dad we would be back to visit later. Since it was a mountainous road, we parked my car by a spring that had a larger parking area. We could see it above the trail where we were hiking.

Benton suddenly remarked, "What is your dad doing under the hood of your car?"

"Oh, he is probably just checking the oil or the other fluids in the car," I replied so innocently and trusting.

Without any warning, the car drove off. My dad and his cousin had hotwired my car and stolen it out from under me. The cousin drove it back to Georgia, but my dad remained behind. We hurried back down the mountain and met my dad at the spring. His truck was parked there. What an overwhelming experience! My heart was both sad and furious

At the Crossroads: A Southern Daughter's Story

at the same time. Once in the truck with my Dad, he headed the truck south, while I hollered and cried hysterically,

> "How could you do such a thing? Why did you take my car? We need to go back to Philadelphia? I love Benton! Why do you try to ruin everything for me? You cannot kidnap me. We both have jobs and have to get back to them."

He finally came to his senses and turned his truck around. I got out at the spring where Benton had remained and where my car had been parked earlier. My dad said nothing, and just headed back to Georgia.

This was a joyless day. The McCanns were nice to open up their home to us, insisting we stay the night. Even though their house had no running water and only an outdoor privy, we were grateful for their kindness after having had such a dreadful, demoralizing day. "The wind had been knocked out of our sails."

Benton said later—"looks like they could throw some lime in that john once in awhile". It did smell terrible but they were used to it and were living off the grid. They did, however, have a telephone. I called my mother, but she didn't seem at all surprised by what had happened. She even asked me to return the ring she had given me that belonged to my grandmother, as well as the title to the car that was given to me the year before graduation.

Another neighbor gave us a ride into Johnson City, Tennessee, where we rented a car to go back to Philadelphia. I told Benton that no one could please my parents, but this was just a poor excuse. The truth was they did not want to let me go. They were terribly possessive. I decided to live my life as best I could. When we returned to Philadelphia, the car deed was signed over and my grandmother's ring was returned—officially disinherited! However, this did not stop angry telephone calls from my mother. She began to call me a "little whore" and denigrate me in other ways. Then she started to say she didn't know why I wanted to marry an Indian.

I said, "Well, Dad met him and he knows that he is not an Indian," I answered.

Angry things were said to her as well. I told her she was on a witch-hunt and her anger was misplaced. Naively a popular book at the time was called *I'm OK, You're OK*, so this was also sent to them by post. We hoped we could develop more understanding for each other, but she returned it to me, signing the inside of the book, "the old witch."

Finishing up my first year of residency was an awfully lonely time for me. Benton and I were not engaged and had not begun to plan a future together. Not having much experience driving in the snow, the car slid into a snow bank. I had an overwhelming feeling of ineptness. Even though a call to Benton would have been a welcome connection, appearing to be a helpless woman, did not sit well with me. Instead, a towing service bailed me out. My parents still called and upset me, so my phone was left unanswered.

Benton became concerned and stopped by one evening to see if I was all right. He still wanted to see me and we discussed the future. He told me he loved me, and hoped we could have a life together. Like his parents, he wanted to work overseas. Benton was quite altruistic, not caring for the material world. He owed some money to the Methodist Church, because as the son of missionaries, he had borrowed the money to study. He also got the GI Bill because of his service as a Green Beret in Viet Nam, but that was not enough. His estimated debt was about $35,000.

I asked him to let my parents get to know him better before he started talking about overseas work. My mom and dad probably could not take it, since I was an only child. Although my parents had adopted a baby when I was 17, they still were selfishly attached to me. It was a hard, complicated predicament trying to please my parents and planning a life with Benton. He kept insisting that my parents needed to know about our plans to leave the United States and work overseas.

By this time, I had become a member of the United Methodist Church. The pastor of the Methodist church had asked for a letter of recommendation from the local Mormon Church I had previously attended. The bishop of the Mormon Church wrote back that they were not familiar with this, and as such could not send a letter to him. The Methodist minister was shocked, even though it was just a formality and courtesy from one church to the other. This was another eye opener for us. The Mormon Church, like so many other Christian Churches, believed it was the only true church of Jesus Christ.

We became engaged in the spring of 1970 and decided we would marry in September over the Labor Day weekend, adding on a few more vacation days. We would marry at his former United Methodist church in Salt Lake City, Utah. No one had offered to help me with my wedding in Georgia, but since we both had friends and I had the Parkers in Salt Lake City, this seemed like a good location. Some of my friends from the Medical College of Georgia were also living in Utah; they offered to help with my wedding. Also Benton's sister, Anna, lived in Utah with her husband and their parents would be on leave from Nepal during this time, staying with them. Anna and James were teaching at Utah State University, while working on their PhDs. We wrote his parents to tell them our news.

They wrote back April 20, 1970

"Our dear Joan,

Your lovely letter to us was very much appreciated and I did answer by return post. We are distressed to learn it never reached you and although Benton has, I am sure told you of our writing, we want to answer you that our response to your letter was warm and with gratitude.

We are indeed very happy and grateful that our son has found a partner for life whom he so deeply loves and respects and we in our turn welcome you most lovingly into our family. We appreciate with you the disappointment of having your parents object but we hope and pray that in time they will become reconciled to the idea.

Meanwhile we rejoice in the thought that you and Benton plan a life together of service and outreach to others and we look forward to your coming out to either Nepal or Afghanistan (both wonderful countries) as the way opens up.

Benton has said that neither of you will be able to get much leave before early September. Naturally, we hope that we can be at your wedding, but we have written to Benton that whatever date you plan, will be OK with us. Do keep us informed about your plans and let us help in any way we can.

There will be lots to talk about when we meet. We'd love to have a picture of you (both of you together if you can)

Thank you for helping Benton with his dislocated shoulder, and for cooking so many delicious meals for him. Our love to you and God's richest blessing.

Affectionately, Mavis Blaskey

At the Crossroads: A Southern Daughter's Story

Benton had been diagnosed with celiac sprue, some years prior to our meeting. He had to be extremely careful of gluten, which seemed to be in about everything, even many ice creams. I was mindful to avoid wheat products and he was sincerely appreciative. Corn bread was a good substitution, so I used to make spoon bread, which he enjoyed.

Benton got his copy of his parents weekly letter addressed to him, his sister and her husband and shared it with me.

April 19, 1970

Dearest Anna, James, and Benton,
The post office, like the rest of the government departments of Kathmandu has been on holiday most of the week. How they run things here I don't know. There was the New Year (Hindu) holiday on Tuesday, the Ram Naumi Wednesday and then because one of the younger princesses got married they closed Thursday and Friday; then Saturday is the usual holiday! The man-hours wasted are really astonishing. So mail is still stacked mountain high in the P.O., and we have nothing from you. I think I shall lead a protest procession to Tundikhel (the royal palace of the king).

The week was particularly busy as Jonathan got back from some committees, and then kept us on the hop with films and correspondence being handed over before his trip to Europe and the USA. He left this morning and will return the day we leave. So I am the "in-charge" at the Headquarters until we start home early June.

Mother kept busy entertaining. We had the Harold family in for dinner Monday evening, and heard all about their hike to Langtang

Khola. Claire Harold seems to have had altitude sickness most of the time and was miserable in the khola; but Tom, the "torn ligament" kid, quickly recovered from his crutches, and eventually got to 16,000 feet!

The Methodist professor from Claremont arrived with wife and daughter Tuesday, and I had to squire them for a while, plus bringing them to tea at the cottage. Mother served a nice tea with scrumptious sponge cake, cream and rhododendron jelly filling.

After a lot of concentrated desk work, especially on completion of the book manuscript for Jonathan to take to London for printing, it was a welcome change to get out on Saturday afternoon to see some of the prize-winning gardens. The American Ambassador's display was exquisite. However, we were the only visitors to the Harold's garden. Their gardener was thrilled!

Sunday, today, was very busy. I was at the early Anglican service and then got back to pick up mother and some Headquarters guests for the Rabi Bhawan service. We had a most interesting and challenging sermon by an American Chemistry professor who spoke on "Smog in the Garden.". It was of course an ecology and pollution sermon, but it was exceedingly well done, and stressed the Christian responsibility in a number or areas. He also stopped halfway through to have a young fellow play his guitar (very skillfully) and sing (splendidly) a Pete Seeger song "It's a garbage dump" [from the song Seventy Miles] —very topical. This evening we went to an Australian teacher's home to baptize his young son.

At the Crossroads: A Southern Daughter's Story

We are hopeful that the mail tomorrow may bring in some letters from your end, for we are eager to hear from you. I hope your hunter-doctors got back to Philadelphia, Benton, and delivered our small parcel to you. We gave it to Dr Burns of Temple University I think.

We love the colour picture Joan sent. It is very good of you and shows Joan to be an exceedingly attractive girl. You both look very happy!

Warmest love to you all,
God bless you. Ever your, Mom and Dad

The Blaskeys seemed such loving, hospitable people. I was so impressed by the warmth in their letter. What a contrast to my parents. How I wished my folks could have been more open-minded and willing at least to see another perspective other than their own. Not knowing what Nepal or Afghanistan would be like, I had my own doubts and fears, but I loved and trusted Benton and was willing to understand his commitments. At 26, I wanted to settle down.

On June 24th I received a post card from my dad. It was of Joseph Smith's Homestead and above the caption he wrote "a great man." He seemed to be getting religious all of a sudden. It read:

Went to Augusta and tried to call you several times. I didn't hear from you on Father's Day. Johnny bought me a bathing suit and we went to Warm Springs. If you are in need of anything right now, I am able to help you. I have been praying for you. Johnny and I have been reading the Bible. Daddy loves you. RJ.

The summer was filled with work and trying to plan a wedding. My parents refused to accept our plans, so I went ahead on my own. Because Benton had been born in India, they insisted I was marrying an Indian. They could not abide my choice in a husband and would definitely not come to the wedding.

One of the Chinese doctors with whom I worked, knew a dressmaker from the Philippines and she did a beautiful job on my dress and veil. The dressmaker sewed some pearls on the bodice and scattered sequins on the shirt; it was dazzling and I felt beautiful as I slipped it on for alterations. Anna arranged for a photographer and flowers. We decided to have a reception after the wedding at the Methodist Church Social Hall. The Blaskeys would have the wedding rehearsal dinner for us.

I probably should not have sent out the usual wedding announcements, but did the traditional thing and saying, "Mr. and Mrs. Raymond Johnson are pleased to announce their daughter…" The invitations were sent one to my parents and all my other relatives. My Grandpa Parker and Zina were excited for us; they even made a trip to Georgia before the wedding to talk to my folks. They did not disclose, how much Benton and I had been slandered during their visit. Unfortunately, we found this out later. Someone in the family should have warned us about their building bitterness. Although many had met Benton, they didn't seem to be able to overcome all the hatred in my family's hearts. They may have unintentionally added fuel to the fire and talked about the "falling away from the Mormon Church" which was tantamount to apostasy. Hate is a poisonous infection, spreading from the mind into the soul. Unhappily, this infection can be extremely contagious.

On August 27th I got another letter from Mavis Blaskey:

> *Dear Benton and Joan,*
> *Thank you for your letters which were awaiting us when we returned last night from Oregon. I am hurrying to reply, even including some of Anna's*

answers in this, as she has had to dash right off to her lab this AM and will not be free to write until later.

Thank you for sending us a copy of the announcement which we think is fine. The little card included is good too, and people will be glad to have your address in Pennsylvania. [My family had been very ugly about our wedding. They did not approve and the Blaskeys knew about this. It was a source of heartbreak for all of us, but we decided to go ahead without their blessing.]

The papers show the temp and humidity in Philadelphia to be very high. I am sorry you are having to do so much packing and moving in the midst of the heat. But it will be so good to have the apartment all ready for you when you return.

Tremendous storms are here in the West have cooled the temperature down. We drove home last night through torrential rain in Idaho and Utah. Oregon is so dry the loggers can work only at night for fear of fires.

Benton, we are so happy that your first corneal transplant was so successful. You are to be congratulated and we are proud of your accomplishment. We are so glad too, Joan, that you think the flash will be good for skin photographs. Hope it fits all right to your camera.

Anna will arrange for the bouquets for the three older bridesmaids and flower baskets for the two younger ones. She and James love doing flowers and are very skillful. They have contacted the florist here, whom they know and are getting the orders for the bouquets. They will be less expensive here than in Salt Lake City and will be packed to go down in their car in a cooler with ice. So, all will be well.

Joan, don't you think it will be suitable for the three older girls to come to the dinner on Friday night? We do not have any idea of their ages but you do as you think best. Will there be ushers to be their escorts too? We can have as many at the dinner as we like just as long as we get the final numbers in 48 hours before the dinner. We would like you both to tell us your preference with the menu. We have the various choices which the Inn gives. We are happy to include the Dr. from SLC too, Benton. You have not told us whether he is single. If he has a wife she should be asked as well. How nice that he will play the music for the wedding.

Our trip to Oregon was a great success. We had a good reunion with the Blaskey family and Anna made many helpful contacts for her and James' future in teaching. They are quite convinced now that they want to move to Oregon to teach in some smaller college. State Universities they think are too large and impersonal.

We look forward to seeing you both on Wednesday September 2nd and will have some time together then the answers to various questions settled. If we are unable to meet the plane, please both of you come directly to the Rodeway Inn (150 W 6th St) so that we can meet.

You are both so busy; we marvel that you are able to get ready for your wedding! But we do hope you can have a little relaxation here for a couple of days before the Great Day.

At the Crossroads: A Southern Daughter's Story

All our love to you both, Mavis and John, Mom and Dad

P.S. We plan to come to SLC by Greyhound Wed afternoon and take the Airport limousine out to meet you, but first we must deposit our suitcases at the Rodeway Inn--so--there is just a chance we may be late. We hope not and we'll look for you either at the plane or at the Inn.

Love, Mavis

It seemed to me the Blaskeys had such a sense of peace. Self worth plays a role in any sort of development or effective mission work. They had this quality and so did Benton. When Benton talked about working in Asia, I think he also wanted to follow in the foot steps of his parents. He wasn't exactly sure where he would be sent. I had come to accept this because I loved him very much.

We were married over the Labor Day holiday and took three extra days off, so we could enjoy a few of them to honeymoon in one of our favorite places, the Teton National Park. We both loved the mountains. Benton had told me when he got back from Viet Nam, he was so happy to be home that he took his sleeping bag, laid it out in the park, enjoying the wilderness under the starry sky.

We decided to go horseback riding to celebrate being back in the Tetons. There were about 10 to 12 people in our excursion into the alpine countryside and we had a full breakfast from the chuck wagon. The cowboys leading the tour were well organized and we were underway for several hours.

After our short honeymoon, we returned to Philadelphia and our routine. It was good that we had furnished our apartment off the Main Line prior to the wedding because his parents stopped over to see us before heading back to Nepal, where they were still working.

By the middle of September, we started getting wedding gifts and letters of congratulations. One such letter came from my great Aunt Melba:

Dear Joan,
   I'm very proud to know I have a new nephew and that you are OK. I think of you very often. There have been some changes over the past year. I'm having some sinus trouble. One of my age has many complaints. I stay busy and Vivian and Marian [granddaughter] are gone every day to school. They leave quite early and it's about five in the evening before they get back. Danny and I are here at home.

   I was down to St Augustine, Florida the last week of July and then we went to North Carolina to see all the folks. Larry [her nephew] has sold out everything of his property and is leaving for the West where he bought all of his girls beautiful homes and had them furnished. His youngest girl Sandy married in the temple and lives in Filmore, Utah. Leonard, his son is a pilot for American Airlines. He lives in California. He has a sweet wife and two little boys.

   I must stop and get supper. In the evenings I mostly look at television. Danny said he is very proud of his new cousin and is looking forward to meeting him. I wish you were closer. Write me and tell me all about yourself.

Much love,
Aunt Melba

At the Crossroads: A Southern Daughter's Story

It was nice to get a newsy letter from my great aunt Melba. After I read it, I became more optimistic, and felt less estranged from my family.

After our marriage, Benton had to go to a national ophthalmology meeting held in Las Vegas. He was presenting a paper on skin and eye diseases, which we had worked on together. Once we fell in love we were not separated much, but while he was away at the meeting, I received a beautifully romantic card and a separate letter from him. One was addressed to Dr. Joan Johnson and the other to Mrs. Benton Blaskey. I was leaning toward changing my professional name to Dr. Joan Blaskey, but had not made it official.

October 5, 1970

Dearest Joan,
I wanted to write you even if it takes a long time to get to you, since we have been married one month today and what a wonderful month it has been. I love you more every day and look forward to many more months and years of life together.

The flight yesterday was fine although the breakfast came at about 10:30. I was famished by the time they brought it. It was a pleasant 76F (dry) here when we arrived. Our rooms were not ready but we had time to sign up for the courses we wanted and look at some of the exhibits. I went swimming for a short time—not enough to get sunburned! John had seen me give you some money for the parking at the airport and when I met him at the pool, he said,

"Say Joan called and the parking was more money than you gave her and she couldn't get out

of the lot." He never misses a chance to crack a joke.

Seriously I hope you got home all right. There is nothing much going on today—mostly for the resting, seeing the exhibits and registration. Tomorrow starts with the papers and courses in the afternoon. I am taking one on therapeutics and another on neuro ophthalmology and one on ultrasound.

I really wish you were here. You would love the room we have and the big swimming pool.

We went to a dinner show last night and saw "Mame" with Juliet Price. I enjoyed it. The gambling goes on all the time, of course, but it hasn't turned me on yet, and I'm too frugal to gamble a dime.

Well, sweetheart, I'm already looking forward to getting back to you. I love you very much,

Benton.

The warmth and comfort Benton had brought to my life was immeasurable. I felt safe in the arms of the man I loved and looked forward to the future we would build together. I was very calm, so I often fell asleep in his arms.

During the summer prior to the wedding, I had received a letter from Ellie Mae:

Dear Joan,

I was so happy to get a letter from you and to know you are doing fine and also the $5.00 you sent me for Mother's Day. You don't know how glad I was to know you was thinking about me on that day. Well, I am doing much better now. I am

At the Crossroads: A Southern Daughter's Story

doing about as well as you could expect for an old lady. All the rest of the family is doing fine. Laurie is still in school. I hope she will soon be out. Joan, I was glad to hear you are planning on getting married soon. I wish you much joy and a happy marriage, hope you are getting a nice husband because I love you and I don't want you to marry no body that won't be nice to you. I know you can't please your mother but you got to live your own life. No body can live it for you. Well, I'm planning on going up to see your mother soon I hope.

I don't go up very much now because I am not able to work like I used to but I do thank the Lord that I am still able to get up and get around and take care of myself. Are you planning on coming home to get married? If you do I will try and see you. Janis is getting married soon, so Marie won't have but one more left. Of course, Laurie live next door to her. Laurie and the family send a hello to you. She says she is going to write you soon. Close with love always, Ellie Mae"

She was sure right about no one being able to please my mother. I somehow had overlooked that my father was getting as possessive and irrational as my mother. I had trusted him, so it was quite a shock when he betrayed me. I did not realize that Mormonism would turn him into a zealot. Radical thoughts can produce radical actions.

And in her eyes, you see nothing. No sign of love behind the tears, cried for no one, a love that should have lasted years

> John Lennon/Paul McCartney

Chapter Nine
Fate of Innocents

After our wedding in Utah, Benton and I had settled into our routine in Philadelphia. Prior to the wedding we had moved our belongings to an apartment in Bryn Mawr, knowing that we would have to return to work immediately. This decision was also made because the Blaskeys planned to visit a few days with us before returning to Nepal. We wanted to show them our place and Benton also bought concert tickets to the Philadelphia Orchestra, conducted by Eugene Ormandy. They performed Beethoven's Ninth Symphony or the Ode to Joy as it is sometimes called. It turned out to be a powerful concert. Richard Wagner once acknowledged Beethoven as the one composer (besides himself) who sought to redeem humanity through the power of art. I know we felt redeemed. Every time I have listened to the Ninth since, it has sent chills up and down my spine, bringing tears to my eyes. The next day his mom and dad were off to visit friends in New York before flying back to Nepal.

We had been married almost two months, and my mother, in her most charming voice, invited us to come for a visit to the farm. We were both very busy, but decided we needed to respond to the invitation. I think we had hoped the visit from the Parkers from Utah had made a difference; however, the Parkers had not called us. In retrospect, since I had been through the temple, they may have considered me an apostate. We were married in the United Methodist Church by my father-in-law and the Parkers had attended our wedding and seemed to rejoice in our happiness. To be an apostate carried its own consequences, about which I was naively uninformed. I had not anticipated any retribution.

We decided to fly down toward the end of October. Benton and I had a direct flight from Philadelphia to Macon. We arrived about 12 noon and while Benton made arrangements to rent a car, I telephoned my parents.

"How are you feeling, Mother," I inquired.

"I am not feeling well," she replied.

"We will be home in a couple of hours," I told her

"Can't you make it faster!" she said

"Well, since you are not feeling well, we will stop on the way and get some lunch, but we will see you soon." And the conversation ended.

We stopped at the Copper Kettle, which was about an hour away from the farm. It was a rural café and on a Saturday was packed with people. Benton remarked, "I think we are slightly overdressed." It was past 1 PM and we were both starving. We both ordered the pork chop dinner with mashed potatoes and peas.

As we drove toward the farm, we enjoyed the countryside with its rolling hills and the crisp autumn air. The roadside shoulders and ditches were surprisingly clean and the grass was still green. I was proud to show him my home turf.

At the Crossroads: A Southern Daughter's Story

We must have arrived about 3 PM. I was surprised that my brother Johnny was nowhere in sight. I guess I had expected a warm welcome from my little brother. I later learned that he had been sent away for the afternoon. Benton had asked what he should call my mother,

"Mother Johnson?" he inquired.

I said, "Whatever you like, see how you feel. See how the visit goes."

When we arrived my mother was lying on the couch. I went over to kiss her since she did not rise from her supine position. She raised her left hand to stop my advance, saying,

"I want to see how you look."

Mother was still under weight, looking a bit unkempt, wearing lounge pajamas; she was not the attractive mom I wanted Benton to meet. My father was not in the room with her when we arrived. There was a man with my mother who was a stranger to me.

Since no one spoke up, we introduced ourselves to the stranger, Mr. McDaniel. My mother pointed to the chairs where she wanted us to sit. She never did look directly at me.

She then said, "Well, did you get your pussy split open?" I was shocked and embarrassed and made no reply.

Benton spoke up and said,

"Mrs. Johnson, we came down here with good intentions."

To which she replied,

"I never invited you to come and I told you I would have a 38 waiting for you."

Benton then said,

"You did invite us to come, but if you don't want us to stay, we will be glad to leave."

Mr. McDaniel interrupted,

"I heard Beatrice tell you not to come," and then we both said, "We will be glad to leave."

Mother then got up to a sitting position with a small revolver in her right hand and fired several shots above Benton's head. We tried to get the weapon away from her, but while we were wrestling my father came in from the kitchen and said,

"What's going on here? What do you mean coming in here and beating my wife?" This was my dad's first appearance in the room.

My father then got the gun and pointed it at Benton. Benton spoke up, trying to be calm and said,

"Mr. Johnson, we just came down here for a visit. Let's sit down and talk this over."

My mother and Mr. McDaniel kept slapping us and cursing, calling me a whore and saying,

"Let the little bitch have what's coming to her!"

My father shouted at me to sit down and instead I ran from the house expecting Benton to follow me. The last thing I saw as I fled was my father still holding the gun, so I thought Benton would be safe. In a split second, my dad caught up with me; he was slapping me around and pulling my hair. I screamed at the top of my lungs for him to stop. I heard two gunshots while I was in the backyard fighting off my father. My mind reeled! He said nothing but we rushed back inside and Benton was lying on the floor. I picked up his head and it was limp.

I cried out,

"Oh, my God, you shot Benton!"

I tried to use the wall phone, which was close by, but they pulled me away. I tried to administer artificial respiration but as I knelt down my mother said,

"Put a chain around her neck."

My father put the chain around my waist but I managed to break loose. I was still being held by both wrists and was being brutally shaken.

Finally, I broke free but my father caught up with me. I kicked him several times in the privates and broke free again, running away from him as fast as I could. I made it across the road to Mr. and Mrs. Jones' store and frantically asked them to call an ambulance. I also asked them to call the sheriff.

After about five minutes my mother walked across the road with a tire iron in her hand. I hid behind the meat cooler in the store. I asked Mrs. Jones not to let Mother come in, because I was afraid she would shoot me. She was still filled with rage and asked Mrs. Jones if she had seen me, but she said she had not. My mother then got some milk and left the store.

The ambulance and sheriff arrived at my parents' house, pronouncing Benton dead at the scene. His body was taken to a local funeral home while I contacted family and friends in Utah, Pennsylvania, N.J. and far away Nepal. It was a task beyond my capacity, but I had to do it. My neighbor, Mrs. Jones was so generous with her home and tried to comfort me as best she could. She was shocked by all that had happened. I called my mother's brother, Earl and his wife. They lived over two hours away and arrived as soon as they could.

I learned later that my brother, who would have been nine at the time, had been sent away for the afternoon to play with friends. There had been a lot of premeditation in the action of my parents.

The sheriff interviewed me at the Jones' store and I tried to remember, word for word, what had happened to Benton and me in the preceding hour or so.

Although in a state of shock, I still had the presence of mind to do one last thing for my beloved. I asked someone to call the Medical College of Georgia, Ophthalmology Dept and tell them my husband was a corneal transplant donor. They would need to send someone to the funeral home to harvest his eyes. He had told me repeatedly,

> "If anything happens to me, be sure my corneas are given for transplant." It was something I had pledged to do for him and many people probably would not understand that I had the presence of mind to do this.

Our tragic story was all over the local news. Some reports even made the national news. Anna and James were with me during those early days after the murder and tried to shield me as much as possible, but we decided to give two interviews, one was with the Philadelphia Inquirer.

"Philadelphia Doctor's Murder in Georgia Was 'Premeditated,' DA There Says", read the headline on October 27th. A staff writer, John Morrison wrote:

At the Crossroads: A Southern Daughter's Story

A Georgia district attorney said last night he believes the slaying of Dr Benton Blaskey, 32, Philadelphia physician, was premeditated."

His mother-in-law Mrs. Beatrice Johnson, 57, has been arrested and charged with the murder.

District Attorney Moody, who will be the prosecutor in the case, also disclosed that Mrs. Johnson's husband, Elmer Raymond Johnson has been charged with aiding and abetting the murder.

Dr. Blaskey, a third-year resident at Wills Eye Hospital was shot twice with a .38-caliber pistol shortly after he and his wife of seven weeks, the former Joan Johnson, 27, also a Philadelphia physician, arrived to visit her parents. He was killed instantly.

Moody, who said he has six Georgia counties in his jurisdiction and had only briefly looked into the case, said he learned the slaying happened "almost instantly" after the Blaskeys arrived at the farmhouse.

"We think it was premeditated," he said.

Moody said the Blaskeys were married September 5th and flew to Macon Saturday morning, rented an auto and drove about 90 miles to the Johnson's farm. The shooting occurred inside the house, Moody said, but a struggle between Johnson and his daughter continued outside the house.

Moody said his office would resist any attempt by the Johnsons to plead insanity. He said he didn't think that would be a valid plea in this case.

Mrs. Johnson was taken yesterday afternoon from the hospital to Laurens County Jail. Her husband remained free.

The suspect was taken to the hospital shortly after the shooting and placed under sedation. She was remanded there over the weekend.

Moody said Mrs. Johnson will be given a preliminary arraignment shortly and then commitment hearing before three justices of the peace to determine if she should be bound over for the grand jury.

Her lawyer may apply for bail before the County Supreme Court, Moody said, but the justices of the peace are not permitted to grant bail in a murder case. Moody said he didn't think Mrs. Johnson had a lawyer yet.

The Sheriff said late yesterday the motive in the shooting is "a puzzle to us." He said he did not question Mrs. Johnson for fear of violating her rights.

Johnson was described by a knowledgeable member of the area community as a "successful farmer, a substantial man in the community." The family had never been in trouble with the law before, authorities said.

Mrs. Blaskey, also a physician, was in seclusion with relatives.

With her was the Rev Haines, pastor of the United Methodist Church, who flew to Georgia after he learned of the tragedy.

The suspect, Mrs. Johnson, was under the care of her family physician while she was in the hospital.

He said he administered sedatives to her there and had been treating her for "female trouble."

He further stated, "Mrs. Johnson appeared very calm and unworried. She didn't discuss the shooting and didn't volunteer any information. I didn't question her because she was under the jurisdiction of the sheriff."

A nurse at the hospital, who helped take care of Mrs. Johnson said that at one point she asked, "What did I do?"

"You don't know?" the nurse said she asked.

Mrs. Johnson appeared to reflect a moment, the nurse said, and then exclaimed, "Oh, that!" The nurse said Mrs. Johnson appeared "kind of vague" but untroubled.

Dr. Benton Blaskey's parents, Canon [an Anglican title] and Mrs. John Blaskey are United Methodist Church missionaries in Nepal. The father had officiated at the Blaskey's wedding in September.

No words could describe my anguish. I had lost everything and everyone—my mom, my dad, and my beloved. I fell down in a heap. Out of this darkness my husband's sister, Anna became a light for my soul. She and James flew to Savannah to be with me at my aunt and uncle's house. She kept saying over and over—"look for the light. We will be there with you as soon as we can." I had to pull myself together and keep going. I was still a doctor and could help people. I could dig myself out of this abyss but it seemed a monumental task.

Some days later, Anna also gave me a book by Rumer Godden, *The River*. It is the story of the tragic death of a little boy named Bogey killed by a snake bite while his older sister

Harriet was playing nearby. The story deals with her remorse and guilt and how Captain John helps her overcome this crisis in her young life.

This book helped me a lot and I later shared it with my psychiatrist. He thought it was a great story. Somehow in my mind he had become Captain John for me. Harriet was despondent over the death of Bogey and Capt John says,

> "We go on being born again and again with each new episode or incident in our lives. With each new happening, perhaps with each person we meet if they are important to us, we must either be born again, or die a little bit; big deaths and little ones, big and little births."

To which Harriet replied,

> "I should think it is better to go on being born again than to die all the time."

> "If we can," Capt. John said, "but it takes a bit of doing. It is called growing, Harriet, and it is often painful and difficult. On the whole, it is very much easier to die."

> "But you didn't," said Harriet.

> "I just managed not to," said Capt John

The River was a wonderful gift to me from Anna. It was filled with empathy and understanding of death and the struggle to see the light again. It would take me years to overcome what had happened. I was beginning to see the "light" by the time I finished my residency; but might never be able to truly understand this tragedy. In the short term my days consisted of just putting one foot in front of the other. How would I survive?

At the Crossroads: A Southern Daughter's Story

My faith in God would sustain me. He would be Father and Mother to me. He would help me find my way, nourishing and healing my soul. I had my patients and this gave my life purpose. But still not knowing how I would ever find my way back to a sense of normalcy.

There were numerous people who helped in my recovery, but the members of the United Methodist Church were responsible for the lion's share of encouragement. They eventually set up a fund to help sponsor my mission to Nepal. For the 5 months that I was in Nepal they deposited a small stipend in my bank account in Philadelphia. It went a long way in keeping me solvent during the fall and winter of 1972-73.

The organist at the church offered to take me on as a student. I learned more in the two years of study with her, than in the previous six years. It was good discipline and eventually we gave several short recitals for the United Methodist congregation. It was a nice accomplishment for both of us and part of my painful recovery.

One of my professors at Penn kept asking me, "How do you do it—how do you keep going forward?" I really did not know how to answer him. He meant well but at times those words pierced, as though it would be better to dig a hole and jump in. My loss had been so heartbreaking that thinking about the future seemed overwhelmingly bleak. I just shrugged my shoulders and smiled whenever he asked, "How do you do it?" One foot in front of the other, the road ahead would be rocky, but I was feeling better. The hole didn't seem so deep anymore.

That pain you feel: that's life. The confusion and fear: that is there to remind you that somewhere out there, is something better and that is worth fighting for.

Sarah Moores

Chapter Ten
Recovering

I did not understand what had happened to me, and perhaps would never really understand it, but wanted to try. What had I done to my parents to deserve such a heinous crime?

> *"Love your enemies,"* Jesus said. "Do good to those who hate you. Bless those who curse you. Pray for those who mistreat you." (Luke: 6 27-28)

Where did this premeditated plot against us come from? Were my father and mother acting out the beating that he had given her so long ago? This had been a family trauma that had been with us forever. How traumatic that Mama Parker stood by and encouraged my dad to give my mother the beating? Were Benton and I mere pawns for them to vent their anger toward each other and us?

Anger is like a bitter root that can smolder, and lead to selfishness with lack of concern for others. Selfishness then requires justification, which bends everything around so that the wrong doers, in the end, are in the right. Such was the case with my parents and the way they slandered Benton and me. We had frustrated my parents' will; they did not get what they wanted. Although, probably deep down, Mom and Dad didn't know exactly what they wanted for themselves or for me, except the control of my life was a priority.

I did not find out until later that my own community had been told that I had married an Indian or a Black man; the story varied depending on who was telling it. Racism was alive and well, at least in my hometown. After my husband's death, my neighbor asked for a photograph of Benton, so that she could show people he had blond hair and blue eyes. This was 1970 when degrading someone to be less than human could justify the action taken.

During this period, Blacks were not members of the Mormon Church and this may have been a factor in the smear campaign of Benton and me. The priesthood of the church did not accept members of the Black race, although it accepted Polynesians and other Asian races. There was no doubt that racism existed in the Mormon faith, although their attitudes about race were generally close to or more progressive than the national average. Even so, racism played a role in my parents' and the community's rationalization of the trauma they unleashed on Benton and me.

Discrimination was so unhealthy that some years later in 1978 the church leaders headed by Spencer W. Kimball declared they had received a revelation instructing them to reverse the racial restriction policy. The change seems to have been prompted at least in part by problems facing mixed race converts in Brazil. The Mormon Church states that it "opposes racism in any form." In 1997, there were over 500,000 black Mormon members mostly from Africa, Brazil and the Caribbean.

While still in Philadelphia I became friends with a patient who told me about blood atonement and the Mormon faith. The details of our conversation are hard for me to recall except he implied Mormons sometimes justified murder because of certain circumstances. I had never heard about it, but later I came across a book by Jerald and Sandra Tanner called *The Changing World of Mormonism,* published in 1981. The chapter on "Blood Atonement" kept me spellbound. "There are sins that can be atoned for by an offering upon an altar much as in ancient days, and there are sins that the blood of a lamb can not remit, but they must be atoned for by the blood of the man." (First published in *Deseret News,* October 1, 1856, p.235). Naturally, every religion has its criminals, but after reading *Under the Banner of God* (2003), I could now see how such crimes could happen in such an unyielding faith as Mormonism.

Krakauer's book dealt with crimes committed in 1984. A young woman and her daughter, age fifteen months, were killed by her two brothers-in-law, as part of a religious "revelation."

As Krakauer states,

> "There is a dark side to religious devotion that is too often ignored or denied. When the subject of religious inspired bloodshed comes up, many Americans immediately think of Islamic fundamentalism, which is to be expected in the wake of the September 11 attacks on New York and Washington. But men have been committing heinous acts in the name of God ever since mankind began believing in deities."

I will always question how little the Parkers of Utah had communicated regarding their visit to my parents' farm. They did not divulge anything about the visit prior to our going, but later told people they had seen a lot of deterioration in both my parents. My mother and father, they said, were saying terrible things about us. They repeated again and again that I had married an Indian or Black. A week or so prior, another woman in the county shot her son-in-law. We knew nothing about any of these things before our visit.

> In *The Changing World of Mormonism*, the Tanners list the Crimes Worthy of Death: Murder, Adultery and Immorality, Stealing (Brigham Young said thieves should have their throats cut), Using the Lord's name in vain, For Not Receiving the Gospel, for Marriage to an African. Furthermore, other offenses included Apostasy, Lying, Condemning or doubting Joseph Smith as a Prophet.

Since I had officially joined the Mormon Church by going through the Temple ceremonies, and then was married in the United Methodist Church, I realized I had committed an apostasy.

Mormonism is a hard religion in so many ways. President Cannon, leader of the Mormon Church, remarked that the Prophet Joseph Smith taught the doctrine that the seed of Cain could not receive the Priesthood. Furthermore, that any white man who mingled his seed with that of Cain should be killed, and thus prevent any of the seed of Cain's coming into possession of the priesthood. This pronouncement was made toward the end of the 19th century and this attitude persisted until 1978 when President Kimball said he had a revelation from God.

I can write about this with some detachment now, but in 1970, I remained in a state of shock for quite some time. I relied on my friends to help me think. By the end of October, my parents-in-law were back at their missionary post in Nepal, 6,000 miles away. My sister-in-law, Anna and her husband James, who were still living in Utah, came to my rescue within a few days of the tragedy. Pastor Haines from my Philadelphia Methodist church and other family friends arrived to comfort me. I was also truly fortunate to have my

Uncle Earl and Aunt Bertha, who decidedly brought me home with them. They had a large home and I, as well as Pastor Haines, Anna and her husband stayed with them until after the cremation and funeral service were performed. We took Benton's remains with us on our flight back to Philadelphia, all the while, still in a state of anxiety and depression, now more appropriately called Post Traumatic Stress Syndrome.

The young married couples of the church paid for the expenses of the pastor and I will always be grateful for their generosity. Everyone at the United Methodist Church was so kind to me.

My life was in shambles. I was a widow with no mother or father. Coming across a poem that spoke to me, I chose to send it along with a Christmas message to some of my aunts and uncles on my father's side.

Dear God,

What can I do?

I can put her away privately,

But nothing is private

In this village.

I cannot do this

To one so young,

So lovely,

So helpless.

I, too, will believe it is

Of God.

I will take her to the land

Of my fathers.

And raise him
As if he were really
My own.

He shall never know
He is not mine.

And Jesus grew in wisdom,
And in strength,
And in favor with God and man.
And when a man,
He described God.
He said,
"God is like a father."

J Frank Bartleson

"Dear family,
As Christmas approaches I know you are wondering how I am and if there is anything you can do for me. Christmas is a time of sharing and loving our family and friends in the spirit that Christ taught us. The poem I have enclosed reminds me of Benton and me.

My life has been a riddle that I've tried to understand. It came to Benton and me last Christmas and this Christmas I want to share it with you.

The story is somehow like a riddle, but if you have compassion you will understand. My mother had no father, my father (he lost his mother as a

At the Crossroads: A Southern Daughter's Story

teenager) had no mother, and they expected me to be both. "I can't," I said, even after we knew. "I've my own life to live and I'm only human. Can't you understand?" but they kept hoping and never could accept, and then one day I did return with my beloved and it was too late. The possession and greed of many generations was in their eyes, and they said, "If we cannot have her, no one else will." They hated me and my beloved because we were different, but we did not know. "What is this difference", some will ask now?

Beauty is in the eye of the beholder, and some see through a glass darkly but never eye to eye. But you CAN learn if you will only try. The Spirit of God dwells within you, and as you help others, you also help yourself. Don't be afraid, and always trust your children as you would trust yourself.

My life will never be the same.
Love, Joan

I was fortunate to have the psychiatric counseling available at the University of Pennsylvania. In fact, I had the chief of the department as my psychiatrist. He seemed pleased with my letter and said he thought it was appropriate for my relatives, but said to be more cautious with your parents-in-law. They have suffered a far greater loss in losing their only son, just when he was close to the pinnacle of his career.

My biggest problem was sleeping, as well as, having general anxiety. Fears that my parents might still hire a "hit man" to kill me would not let my mind rest. The prescription medications helped and my doctor recommended a lot of physical exercise to improve my sleep. I started swimming three or four times a week. Christmas was going to be especially hard, but my sister-in-law, Anna, and her husband, James, suggested that we should bring the senior Blaskeys back from Nepal, so we could be together in Logan, Utah, where they lived and were teaching. We needed to be together for Christmas to begin to heal. The whole family was so supportive of me. It was the best decision to have the Blaskeys home for the holidays; it proved to be therapeutic for all of us. Out of this terrible tragedy, we hoped to create something good. I just remember being enveloped in love, nourished both physically and spiritually.

The Blaskeys were the fourth generation in their family to work in Asia. In many ways, they were the last vestiges of the missionary aristocracy that was uniquely British and some leftover colonialism. Although the life as a foreign missionary had its drawbacks, it also carried its privileges. A missionary suffered a few slings and arrows, mostly of the digestive system, but nowhere else could a worker have a cook, a gardener and a cleaning lady. Mavis' grandfather had been a bishop in India and she spoke Hindi like a native. My father-in-law was also quite proficient in Hindi, but she was the one who commanded the servants and gave the orders. Mavis was quite precise, had a good disposition, always smiled and never lost her temper. John was quiet and well disposed, which is why he was such an asset to the United Mission Headquarters and held the title of Assistant Executive Secretary of Correspondence.

The Blaskeys' move to Nepal was a way of easing them into retirement. He had been headmaster of the international school, called Woodstock School, which was situated in the foothills of the Himalayan Mountains in a city called Mussoorie. It was where Benton was born in 1938. Located about 160 miles north of Delhi, it appeared to be built on the side of a mountain, and lay at an altitude of 6,000 feet. The school was somewhat of an elitist institution; even in the sixties, the tuition was several thousand dollars. It had the support of the various Protestant Churches and Missions: Presbyterians, Methodists, United Church of Canada, as well as Baptists, Mennonites and Assemblies of God. One of its missions was to foster a greater understanding of Indian culture, history, art, and music.

Americans made up about 20% of the student body with the rest coming from Canada, India, and the United Kingdom. It was a boarding school and the students were children of missionaries or government workers from the State Department. The teaching staff was similarly mixed with various nationalities. Benton often spoke fondly of his days there and thought it was the greatest school imaginable because of its cultural diversity. He also spoke fluent Hindi and Urdu.

Mavis taught English and drama. She also wrote beautiful poetry and demonstrated this poetic tendency in their yearbook, *The Whispering Pine*.

> *To the great scholars of antiquity, inspiration came from the skies and the breezes, from the music of running water, and the delicate colors of flowers, and trees. So I have been set thinking of our time as scholars. Then quoting Henry David Thoreau: 'If you built castles in the air, your work need not be lost; that is where they should be built; now put foundations under them.' Let us listen to the voice of the wise man who says, 'Do not live to make a living; rather live to make a life'.*

What a powerful message for a graduating class.

I was exceedingly fortunate to have the Blaskeys in my life. After Christmas vacation, John and Mavis accompanied me back to Philadelphia. There we gave several talks at the University Hospitals and in the churches about Nepal, stressing the need for aid to the country through this unique organization known as the United Mission to Nepal. We wanted to make some good out of our tragic loss, so decided to show a film to the various groups where Benton had worked. The documentary was called "On the Potter's Wheel."

This film was an excellent production with the Himalayas as its backdrop. The feature demonstrated the primitive way the Nepalese lived using tools that the Western world had used in the 17th and 18th centuries. Their lack of transportation was a particular hardship, and often meant traveling for days by foot, or in a gurney carried by two able bodied persons if one was too sick to walk. The Himalayas were breathtakingly beautiful with Mount Everest as its focal point, the tallest mountain in the world. It gave Nepal a distinction no other country could boast, but the tourism that it promoted had not helped to modernize the countryside. In some respects, it just polluted Nepal with trash, including numerous empty oxygen containers as many climbers made their way to various peaks, including Mount Everest.

Many Tibetans also lived in Nepal, and the Sherpa were the most well known for being skilled guides for the treks in the Himalayas. Many other tribes of Nepalese still followed their own trades and customs, among them the Newars, who were wood carvers and potters. Unfortunately these people heated their houses with wood or dried cow dung, so there were many respiratory ailments, including tuberculosis. However, most of the natives suffered from chronic bronchitis. Malnutrition and poor water supplies lead to cholera, diphtheria, and all sorts of parasites, malaria and leprosy. The way of life for the ordinary Nepalese was covered in the film.

During the presentations, which my father-in-law and I gave, I was mainly responsible for introducing him as the speaker, and sharing some of Benton's and my philosophy of medicine by quoting Albert Schweitzer's book, *The Light Within*:

> *Anyone can rescue his human life, in spite of his professional life, who seizes every opportunity of being a man by means of personal action. Such a man enlists in the service of the spiritual and good. No fate can prevent a man from giving to others this direct human service side by side with his life's work.*

I had often asked Benton about Nepal. Why Nepal? Why Asia? Why Viet Nam? Why must America give so much? And his answer was that our country has so much to give. Since our country is the richest and most powerful country in the world, we must help the less fortunate people of the world. I later discovered that it is only in reaching out to others that we "find ourselves" and can have a new perspective on our problems at home.

Benton thought at times Americans had too much Yankee ingenuity—telling the people abroad how they can improve their conditions rapidly. Americans have not learned the virtue of patience or the value of learning from Eastern culture.

Many developing countries had bad experiences with Christian missions and so the Nepali government asked to have a United Mission Organization, where certain proselytizing standards were discouraged. In this organization were Catholics, Protestants and Pentecostals, and development workers from Bread for the World, Service Overseas out of Germany and other western aid organizations. The Mennonites also sent their PAX (peace) men to this mission as an alternative service to serving in Viet Nam. The United Mission was really a religious melting pot.

Shortly after arriving at the United Mission to Nepal, I had the opportunity to attend a general conference for the mission. During a conference meeting, someone started speaking in tongues. The speech sounded as though it was Scandinavian; I thought the man was talking in his native tongue. A Swedish girl sitting next to me, quickly clarified that this was not the case—the Spirit had taken hold of him.

Life has no blessing like a prudent friend.

Euripides

Chapter Eleven
Jurisprudence

I was confused about the legal proceedings and what was required of me in this terrible tragedy.

Having retained an attorney in Georgia, my father-in-law, John Blaskey, made it clear that I did not need to have an attorney. Benton and I were the victims, and as such, the State of Georgia would be carrying the burden of prosecution.

Without my husband's family and the help of so many good people in my church, I could not have maintained my sanity. My dear friend, Millicent, a fellow member of the Methodist Church, became like a second mother to me, contributing tremendously to my recovery. She was a prudent friend.

She always wrote from the heart, telling me what I needed to hear. I was so touched by her letter of condolence, after the church service in Philadelphia:

At the Crossroads: A Southern Daughter's Story

October 30, 1970

Joan, dear,

You have been so much in my thoughts and prayers all week, and then when I went to tell you so last night, I was too sympathetic to do so! You did such an excellent job getting through the service, and I could just know God was giving you the grace and stamina to maintain such composure—as he did to me when I lost my husband just a little over a year ago. It is remarkable what we are able to do with his help, and one of the most comforting things is to know that we are never alone—that he is always in the room with us, or walking with us on the street, or at work. My friend Ruth, a fellow church member, is such a kind person, and she had such strength when she faced the loss of her husband.

You are wise going back to work as soon as you are able. Keeping busy helps one to make the adjustment. I redecorated my apartment, retired from the government service, and started working at the Law School at Penn. It has all been so good for me, for I love working for these two professors—they are fine men.

When you are able and free to come, I'd love to have you come in for dinner—on a Saturday or Sunday, perhaps.

I am enclosing a check for you to add to Benton's memorial fund. That is such a fine idea! It will be a great tribute to the esteem his friends, co-workers, and family held of him, and it will be a comfort to you also.

Jean Gotlieb Bradley

Please call upon me if I can be of any help to you, Joan, and I shall continue to ask God to give you strength and grace to face each day at a time—He will.

With Love, Millicent

She was of Swedish ancestry and projected a feeling of serenity and reassurance. I latched on to her and she never failed me. She was a widow with a married son. There was sufficient room in her life, both literally and figuratively, for me. I stayed in her extra bedroom for over a month sharing meals. She helped so much to mend my wasting body and broken spirit.

She looked Swedish with her blonde hair, sparkling blue eyes and small dimples in her cheeks. Millicent was slightly overweight, wore knit suits and orthopedic shoes, giving the appearance of an old-fashioned executive secretary. Without her, I don't think my recovery from this terrible trauma would have been as quick, or as strong. She was and remains to this day a significant person in my life. She helped me to grow and overcome my loss.

Millicent had gone to Washington, DC before WWII and worked for the Department of Justice and the Securities and Exchange Commission. She married Ted during this period, and they had a son a few years younger than me. When I came to know Millicent, she was very active in the Methodist Church; we started sitting together during the services. She shared the birthday date January 11th of my father and the birth year of my mother, 1914. Millicent was everything they weren't: contemplative, cheerful and not impulsive. During my last two years in Philadelphia, she was a calming influence and gave me respite from my agony.

Within a month, I rented a room from her neighbor across the street. We were still able to share frequent meals, but it gave us both more space. Another lifesaver was a young lawyer who worked for the Defenders Association of Philadelphia. Millicent introduced me to Stuart, who was also a member of our Methodist Church.

It had been many months since Benton's murder and Stuart could not believe that no one from Georgia had made any contact with me. I was in limbo.

Stuart wrote several letters on my behalf.

May 14, 1971, a letter was sent to the Superior Courts Judicial Circuit where the crime took place.

> *Re: State of Georgia vs Johnson, Johnson and McDaniel*
>
> *I appreciated speaking with you again recently concerning the above matter.*
>
> *Doctor Blaskey is under the impression that you will require her testimony before the Grand Jury in June. She will continue to cooperate with you and will be present when you want her.*
>
> *Would you please let us know, as soon as possible, the date, time and place so that Doctor Blaskey can make the necessary arrangements.*
>
> *Very truly yours,*
> *Stuart James*

No one replied to this letter. Nothing had happened in the case of the State of Georgia vs my parents and Mr. McDaniel. Pastor Haines of the Methodist Church finally wrote a letter to then Governor of Georgia, Jimmy Carter. (I never will forget that his reply arrived postage due!) The Governor wrote the usual stuff you would expect to hear—justice will be done and the letter was forwarded onto his Assistant Executive Counsel.

In September 1971 my friend wrote a letter to the same District Attorney in charge of the case.

> *"Because of your failure to communicate with Doctor Blaskey and me on the above matter, we were forced to call the Governor's office. I understand from that office that you plan to present these cases to the Grand Jury on the second Monday of October and to proceed to trial immediately thereafter. If so, would you please write or telephone me to confirm the arrangements.*
>
> *The long delay in bringing this matter to trial has caused Doctor Blaskey much anxiety, concern and inconvenience. The longer it goes the more difficult it is for her. I appeal to you to please expedite this matter so that it can be completely disposed of without further delay."*

This letter was followed up with several phone calls that were ignored, so Stuart finally spoke with the Executive Office again and we at last got a response from the local District Attorney's office.

In late September 1971, he replied:

> *The Grand Jury will convene on the Second Monday in October Superior Court. It will be necessary for Dr. Blaskey to be present in Court by ten A.M. on that date. Dr. Blaskey's mother remains a patient in Central State Hospital which is a hospital for the treatment of the mentally ill. I cannot assure you and Dr. Blaskey that we will be able to go to trial on the case involving her mother due to her commitment. However, many months ago I suggested that you have Dr. Joan*

At the Crossroads: A Southern Daughter's Story

Blaskey talk with her mother's doctor so that she could assure herself and inform me of her opinion of her mother's condition. (Neither Stuart, nor I, remembered any such conversation, furthermore, it would not have been appropriate). To date I have heard nothing from you in this regard. But regardless of her mother's condition we can still proceed with the Grand Jury phase of this case.

I would like to bring to your and Dr. Blaskey's attention again that this Office cannot and will not be responsible for any item of expense incurred by Dr. Blaskey in attending the Superior Court in connection with this case inasmuch as there is no authority for the authorization of such expenses by this office. However, I do understand that she received a letter from the County Attorney which does on behalf of the County Commissioner authorize a limited reimbursement of expenses.

Very truly yours,
District Attorney Moody

Stuart sent me a copy of the letter with a personal note,

"Joan, Received this today—I can't believe it! Call me."

This gave me only a few weeks to prepare and once again the pastor of my church and his wife came to my rescue and accompanied me to this hearing in October.

They went with me to Georgia along with another family friend. We flew down to Macon, rented a car and were present for the convening of the Grand Jury. I was anxious and tried to answer their questions, tapping the events in my memory. It was surprising to me that one of the women on the Grand Jury wanted to know if there had been contact with my mother since the murder. Shocked by the question, a simple "No" answer was given. Neither Stuart nor I heard anymore from the county or the District Attorney until over a year later.

We had all seen how the wheels of justice were grinding and finally Benton's parents lovingly told me, that they did not expect me to put my life on hold for the State of Georgia. It had been a year and a half since my husband's murder, and the circumstances continued to be traumatic for me. My residency in dermatology would be finished the following summer. I had decided, when my program was completed, to go to Nepal. It was not the most likely place the Board of Missions planned to send Benton, but his parents, John and Mavis Blaskey, were still there and this made me feel more secure. I did not want to sign up for an extended stay without knowing more about Nepal.

Benton had been in correspondence with the Board of Missions of the United Methodist Church in NYC. One such letter he received was quite wordy and talked about his going to Kabul, Afghanistan. There was an ophthalmology hospital, which had been started with the help of a German doctor. The most common eye disease was trachoma, a chronic conjunctivitis, caused by Chlamydia resulted eventually in blindness. Ophthalmology was such a great field of study; an ophthalmologist could actually make the blind see!

I had heard of a volunteer group of physicians called American Doctor located in California. They sent physicians to over 50 countries in the world, and Nepal was among them. Generally, the volunteer doctors helped supply coverage for vacations or provided skills that otherwise were not available.

It was nice for me to have an umbrella organization, and American Doctor corresponded for me to the Chief of Staff at the hospital. Nepal had only one or two dermatologists in the whole country; the hospital asked me to set up a clinic for skin diseases.

The senior Blaskeys were still in Nepal and they were so wonderful to me, making me feel like a real daughter. Every week I received a "round robin" letter from them along with their daughter Anna and her husband James. They had so much love in their hearts, even though we all had sustained such a horrible tragedy. Without their love, recovery would have been impossible. Their letters and encouragement were like a lifeline. I wrote them every week, "Dear Mom and Dad" and kept them up to date about my plans to come to Nepal. My dear friend, Millicent, let me use her address for forwarding mail, since I planned to be out of the country for at least five or six months. The Board of Dermatology required a year of practice before one was eligible to stand for certification, so a return to the States was planned during the following winter to begin preparations of intense study for this difficult examination.

Arriving in Nepal in September, the air was cool and crisp with no monsoon rains. I started my work at the Shanta Bhawan Hospital. A small apartment had been arranged for me on the top floor of an old Rana's palace, which was part of the hospital. It was where they housed some nurses and visiting doctors.

I had never seen such poverty with open sewers and few paved roads. So many people carried large baskets strapped to their heads and looked like beasts of burden. In a Hindu country, cows are sacred and often roam the city unattended. The cow dung was saved then, made into large flat pies. These were dried on the sides of buildings to be used as fuel for cooking. Many people earned only a dollar a day.

It has been said of Nepal, that it has more temples than houses and more gods than people. Since it is primarily a Hindu and Buddhist country, there are numerous temples, shrines, and Stupas which house revered relics. Many monasteries, pilgrimage sites, and statues of divine beings can be seen throughout the countryside. There was a mythical atmosphere; this probably came from the Tantric teachings of both Hinduism and Buddhism. Tantra is a Sanskrit expression that loosely denotes a body of sacred literature, incorporating teachings that give guidance toward release from the chain of rebirth.

One of the most striking of their religious items of worship is the Tanka. The Blaskeys had a Tibetan Tanka. It was a painting on cloth that hung like a scroll with silk brocade surrounding an elaborate Buddha. Though the religious symbolism might escape a Westerner, anybody looking at this colorful banner is struck by its beauty. A picture of the Buddha was drawn in glowing colors forming the center, which was then surrounded by dark blue silk material, richly decorated with star motifs. Around the central figure, there are rows upon rows of godlike figures, all of them different, in various poses, clad in different colored robes and headdresses. Each one carried a bowl, a sword or candleholders. Their facial expressions differed, some smiled, some looked grim. All of the images were overpowered by the impressive Buddha in the middle.

The first time I saw a Tibetan banner or Tanka, it filled me with a mixed emotions, which even now are hard to verbalize; I think this ambivalence came from lack of understanding. It is easy to judge other religions, especially, when they seem so foreign. A Catholic priest routinely prays for the pagans of the world. At the same time, an outsider entering a Catholic church might feel it was not a monotheistic religion as one gazed at all the statues of the saints and apostles. Seldom do we ask questions about what is familiar and commonplace to

At the Crossroads: A Southern Daughter's Story

ourselves. I learned a tremendous amount from the Blaskeys about world religions. They had traveled so extensively and were so well educated. They were devout Christians but had open minds. Their faith was strong enough not to be intimidated in learning about other spiritual paths.

Millicent longed to go to Europe, so before flying to Nepal, we planned to see Europe. She had never been to her ancestral country of Sweden, so she and another good friend of ours, Marla, all traveled around for three weeks. We visited England, Scotland and the Scandinavian countries. It was such a wonderful experience for us—I was the designated driver when we weren't on a bus tour. We covered lots of territory and souvenir shops. Remaining in contact with my Aunt Bertha and Uncle Earl, postcards were sent to them along the way.

After I got to Nepal, some mail awaited me.

October 16, 1972

Dear Joan,

We hope everything is fine with you today. We had a very light shower last night. We are losing some of our plants. On Friday October 6th I received a subpoena to appear in court on Monday the 9th. That night we called the Sheriff and asked to get excused but were not given the privilege. He said he had tried to locate your lawyer and couldn't. Then he contacted the hospital and someone there told him you were in Nepal practicing medicine. He also said Beatrice was insane at the time of the murder but was well now and they were going to get the case over on Monday. He inferred that she would be freed at that time. Sunday night we called your friend Millicent and informed her of the court's decision and asked her if you had left orders for your lawyer in case of something like this. She said she would check with him.

But before this call to Millicent, your dad called and asked if I would be in court on Monday. I told him that I had no alternative. He said Beatrice had been brought down for the trial. I asked him where she was and he said "somewhere nearby" but would not say where. The Sheriff had already told us that she was in the jail awaiting the trial.

I reported to the courthouse around 9 AM and around 10 AM your parents, their lawyer and the Sheriff came in and went straight for the defense table and sat down. Judge Conn came in after this and made a few preliminary announcements and declared that court was in session. It took until noon to draw a jury. We were excused until 1:30 PM and all witnesses were removed from the courtroom and placed in a room with a bailiff. Some I did not know. The doctor was the first one to be called and then about 4 other doctors were called one at a time, but all did not witness. We were still in the witness room when the verdict was read. Beatrice was cleared of the murder charge due to insanity but was returned to the mental hospital. It seems the charges against your dad and Mr. McDaniel were dropped. We heard that Beatrice may be released within a few days, but Earl thinks it will be longer.

Earl's political opposition is fighting harder and harder. He has to be out almost every night to try and keep things in line. The NAACP from Savannah and neighboring towns is here working against Earl. We still think we can win but I have *made up my mind that whatever happens here will be for the best.*

I am getting a good start at school now. (She taught the 1st grade) The hardest part is over, now that the students are getting settled in their routine.

Darrell, my brother-in-law is losing ground with his cancer. He is back at Emory Hospital. Trina (her sister) called me yesterday. Earl and Darrell have gotten real close.

We think of you very often and wish we could call and talk but since we can't, writing will have to do. Write when you can.

Love, Aunt Bertha and Uncle Earl

On November 19th another short letter arrived from Aunt Bertha

Dear Joan,
This is the first Sunday in a long time that we have been at home alone. Willis and family were here the weekend of Nov 3-5 but several of them were sick. Darrell, my brother-in-law died on Nov 4th and was buried the 6th the day before the election. Earl and Darrell were so close that it was like losing a brother. I'm afraid Earl will not want to go back up there much any more and I do need to see my mother as often as possible. We had an announced write-in candidate who worked hard to defeat Earl in the county school superintendent race but we worked hard, had good support from the teachers and won without much difficulty. It was 3:1 margin. Our friends Shirley and Martha gave us a "victory dinner" at Shirley's house. We had turkey and all the trimmings. It reminded us

of your Thanksgiving dinner last year. We miss you and will be thinking of you this year. We will be in Alabama with the children.

During Darrell's illness we went to Dublin and Atlanta often. We passed your home several times and the Oldsmobile was parked at the back steps (it had never been there before) so I felt like Beatrice was at home but we never stopped anywhere near until last Sunday when we stopped at Vivian's and saw your great Aunt Melba. She told us that Beatrice had been coming home for several weekends but went back on Sunday night to the State Hospital.

I hope someday Earl can understand the nervous feeling I have. We have been married 33 years and I have had enough. Love, Aunt Bertha

By the middle of November, I had been in Nepal for over two months. The Blaskeys were in the States visiting Anna and James, planning to return after Christmas. I continued to work at the hospital clinic, and to give full time missionaries a break. I even did some general medicine in outlying facilities on a few weekends.

I had resigned myself to the situation in Georgia. My life was in a different community now, and not just by being physically located in Nepal, but being a different place emotionally than I had been in Georgia so many years ago. The hurt had been so deep that for self-preservation, I had to expand my horizons and not think about my dreadful ordeal. Meeting other people my age helped a lot. During this time Karsten Gottlieb came into my life.

Though I know I'll never lose affection for people and things that went before, I know I'll often stop and think about them. In my life I love you more.

John Lennon/Paul McCartney

Chapter Twelve
In the Himalayas

From the rooftop of my apartment in the old palace, there was a panoramic view of the Himalayan Mountains. The hospital had a nursing school and most of the students lived on the second floor. I lived on the third floor and there were at least two other living quarters on the north wing of the building, where nursing administrators resided. Although there was a bathroom and a kitchen sink, one of the major drawbacks to the apartment was its lack of running water. Luckily, a woman looking for work contacted me, and turned out to be a lifesaver. She carried buckets of water to the top floor for me, and with her help, this inconvenience turned out to be of little consequence. All drinking, cooking, and cleanup water had to be boiled. There was a two-burner hotplate, as well as a nice selection of clay pottery in which to store the potable water.

I held a dermatology clinic three days a week at the Shanta Bhawan Hospital doing my best with the limited supplies that I had shipped to Nepal. Sending anything there was tricky—rats or rogues helped themselves to many useful items in the supplies. By the 1970's, disposable syringes with needles were the norm of the times, but a few doctors donated somewhat obsolete items to me for the mission. Mailing such things to Nepal was prohibitively expensive. I thanked them but never bothered to take them along. Even in Nepal, stainless steel needles that had been re-sterilized and sharpened were often of little use.

Fortunately, the hospital had a good pathology department that helped in doing examination of tissue samples. The interpreters they provided were also excellent and bridged the language barrier. At the mission language school I started to learn some Nepali. This worked out well because after three weeks, one had some working knowledge of the language, could converse a bit with patients and could order things at the bazaar. It was exceedingly difficult to learn with any real proficiency, since the script comes from Sanskrit; it was easier to learn to speak, than write Nepali. This is probably true of any foreign language, but a different alphabet makes writing even harder.

Two Swedish women: Anette, an obstetrician, and Ingrid, a nurse, became good friends of mine. They were extremely devout Christians of the Pentecostal faith, most cheerful and fun to be around. I joined them one weekend for a visit to the leprosy village of Anadaban which was located several hours away from the hospital. We undertook the venture in a trusted Land Rover with few creature comforts; it was a bumpy ride and we were tired by the end of our journey.

The clinic was situated in the foothills of the Kathmandu Valley with seemingly endless expanses of terraces that allowed more room for cultivation of crops. The Nepalese grew rice in the summer and wheat or mustard in the winter. The sweeping contoured terrain with its colorful yellow and green winter crops was a magnificent sight.

We stayed with the Harrison family, and it was amazing how many conveniences they had in this remote area. This, of course, was due to the development work done by the

United Mission. Electricity was available from dusk until 10PM. The lights started flickering around 9:45PM, so there was enough time to light your kerosene lamp. They cooked mainly on wood stoves and supplies were periodically brought in from Kathmandu.

Nepal had a lot of lepromatous leprosy. The other form is called tuberculoid; like tuberculosis, the disease is caused by a spirochete. Leprosy causes major damage to the nerve endings of the hands and feet. Once afflicted by the disease, the patients do not feel any pain or pressure in these appendages. The patients who suffered from leprosy were taught how to protect themselves. Good use was made of old tires that were uniquely crafted into sandals for the patients.

Dr. Harrison occasionally had some trying times with the police. No one was allowed to proselytize the Christian faith in Nepal and they had strict enforcement laws. Most of the population was Hindu or Buddhist, so all denominations of Christians had to show by actions rather than prayer meetings what it meant to be a Christian. Anyway, Dr. Harrison was arrested for supposedly stealing statues or images of various Hindu gods and goddesses. He spent ten days in jail and the police came to search his house and the hospital. It was later disclosed that two men had been beaten up to give false testimony against him. His accusers finally confessed, the statues were found and the doctor released. The police never did identify who was behind this plot to discredit Dr. Harrison.

I had heard about Karsten Gottlieb long before meeting him. Because of his travels he was often mentioned in prayer and was on the Swedish women's prayer list. Gottlieb was from Western Germany and was traveling to Calcutta to claim his Volkswagen bug, which he had shipped over from Europe.

The roads were not so good and he didn't speak Hindi, so everyone was worried because he had been gone for over a week. Communication was poor in rural India and Nepal, and no one had heard from him. Remaining in contact was the biggest problem. A hotel clerk would take a message to send by telex and nod, telling you "right away," but the truth was the hotel had no capacity to send the telex. Culturally it was important not to "lose face." The hotel staff would never think of saying, "Sorry we cannot do this."

After being in language school for a few weeks, one day I looked up and there was Karsten sitting across from me in the circle we had formed. He had a strong German accent and was quite handsome. Quiet, but self-assured, standing almost 6 foot tall, he had soft brown eyes and wavy brown hair. His smile was infectious and friendly. Some weeks later he made an appearance at the dermatology clinic at the hospital becoming a patient.

The process of learning to be a master furniture craftsman in Germany was entirely different from the process in the USA. After middle school in Germany, there was a requirement of four years of integrated classroom study, followed by five years of practicum. Karsten was hired to develop furniture that the Nepalese could easily manufacture to ship around the country and overseas. He had also developed some wood glue allergies, so he was always looking for ways to minimize exposure. Teaching at the Butwal Technical Institute was appealing to him on many levels and because of the allergies he hoped to study "Innen Architektur" (Interior Architecture) when he returned to Germany in a few years.

Karsten came from a good Christian family. He was the youngest son of seven children. He desperately wanted to get out into the world, saying, "My mother could not refuse mission work!"

Although Germany has mainly two Christian denominations, Lutheran and Catholic, Karsten's family had been Methodists for several generations. He had a good job with Service Overseas of Germany as a development worker, so he did not need to constantly look for funding from the church.

Looking back, the Germans seemed to be viewed as not "holy" enough for the United Mission, which may sound strange, but they drank beer and loved to laugh and have a good time. This was probably not appealing to the more fundamentalist Christians. However, the missionaries were always friendly; there was an atmosphere of cooperation between the various trade schools that included a plywood factory, hydroelectric works, an electrical shop, a sales department, and the wood shop where the furniture was designed and built.

The United Mission highly valued the European technology and craftsmanship that these missionaries and development workers brought to Nepal. The system of education in Europe, especially in Germany, was and still continues to be apprenticeships with industry, technical schools and trade guilds. German companies train and pay hundreds of thousands of apprentices every year. Few places in the world can compare.

One of my first encounters with Karsten was over a chair. He was doing a survey about his "giri" chair. Questions such as: do you find the backrest high enough? Is the seat comfortable? Are the armrests high enough? He interviewed a lot of people, but this gave us a chance to get better acquainted. I found him charming and serious about his work.

He knew that I was the Blaskeys' daughter-in-law and I asked him what else he knew about me. His answer surprised me, and was heartfelt, "Many say you have not had an easy life." He was quite sympathetic and invited me to an afternoon of bicycling. We visited some of the Buddhists shrines including Swayambhunath, Kathmandu's most sacred site and the Bodnath Stupa with its outer wall of prayer wheels, which were constantly being touched and turned by pilgrims sending their prayers to the heavens. Under the domes among the statues, women "made puja," and gave offerings. Most of these consisted of necklaces made from marigolds, poinsettia or flowers and rice arranged on a leaf.

Many Tibetans lived in the surrounding community. We went on many such sightseeing tours and picnics, slowly getting to know each other, but I had the feeling of being pursued. On one such outing, it was becoming clearer that we shared mutual feelings for one another. He was always sensitive to my emotions, and as we had our first kiss my heart was filled with joy. I was not used to being so vigorously sought after and it was quite satisfying. Our backgrounds and cultures were different; however, we knew we didn't want to lose what we had.

With so many temples and shrines in the Kathmandu valley, it was easy to think about meditation. We started to read from Christian daily devotions when we were together, sitting on the floor in front of a wooden cross, meditating silently to relax. These quiet times of ours would help to figure out if there was a future for us.

In the evenings I often fixed simple meals. Canned cheese and soups were staples in the kitchen, allowing me to prepare a menu of grilled cheese sandwiches with tomato soup. The evenings were growing cool, and this combination tasted good to us. Karsten spoke fondly about his family, so within a few weeks all their names, their spouses' names and most of the children were familiar to me. I could just feel by the way he talked that he was filled with the same love and pride for his family that I had witnessed with the Blaskeys. I felt fortunate to experience it with Karsten.

I started spending some time on my artwork. My father-in-law was quite good at pen and ink drawings and watercolor, encouraging me in my artistic endeavors. In the Kathmandu Valley, there were artisans who made woodblocks and copper reliefs of drawings. I decided to make my Christmas card using this technique, calling my drawing "Window Tree, Thapathali."

Tahpathali was the hill where the mission was located. The drawing showed a tree growing by a wall with mountains in the background, the Blaskeys' cottage, a pagoda, and minaret in the foreground. It was an amateur attempt, but there were high praises for it and Karsten asked if he could have some cards for Christmas mail to Germany. How flattering!

Soon the Nepali language course would be over and Karsten would have to return to the Technical Institute, which was four to five hours away in the flat Terai area of Nepal on the Indian border. This area of Nepal was hot, like a jungle, a sharp contrast to the Himalayan Mountains. It was also near the area where Siddhartha Gautama lived and died, the "enlightened one," later known as Buddha, who became the spiritual master of one-third of mankind. In Nepal there is to a large extent a fusion of the two religions—Hindu and Buddhism. We wanted to make a trip to Lumbini where Gautama was born in 560 B.C. but never accomplished it.

I had made arrangements to visit a small mountain hospital in Tansen and this was only about one and a half hours from his headquarters. Bus transportation was available, but there was a lot of walking to catch it from this hospital, which was built into the hillside. The hospital saved many lives; it had a good reputation among the natives. People often traveled for days with a sick or injured relative in high hopes the medical staff could perform a miracle. No meals were provided for the patients. Instead, small huts were located on the grounds, where the family cooked meals for themselves and the hospitalized relative.

After a few days of touring the hospital, Karsten arranged for me to visit him over Christmas; I stayed at the Guest Quarters. Now it was his turn to fix us simple meals. They were impressive! His sister had sent him care packages regularly, so he had coffee, tea, chocolate, as well as noodles and various sauces to offer. He also had porcelain cups and saucers along with several nice glasses—a real gentleman.

One of the most striking discoveries, when I visited his small apartment, was his choice of reading material. Even though it was mostly all in German, I noticed right away there was a book on his bedside table called,

Das Innerlichen Licht, or *The Light Within* by Albert Schweitzer. This was a book I had seen often at Benton's apartment.

Schweitzer's words were in the original German, but it was the exact same book I had seen before. Karsten translated many of his thoughts for me:

> *It became steadily clearer to me that I had not the inward right to take as a matter of fact any happy youth, good health, or my power to work. Out of the depths of my feeling of happiness there grew up gradually within me an understanding of the saying of Jesus that we must not treat our lives as being for ourselves alone. Whoever is spared personal pain must feel himself called to help in diminishing the pain of others. We all carry our share of the misery which lies upon the world.*

And yet another beautiful thought:

> *Sometimes our own light goes out and is rekindled by a spark from another person. Each of us has cause to think with deep gratitude of those who have lighted the flame within us.*

Karsten was kind and affectionate and we were falling in love. He was so tender, nothing was ever rushed. I knew that in spite of my plans to leave Nepal in January, and return to the States, our paths would be crossing again. I was blessed once more with a good man.

In January, after being in Nepal for months, I flew back to the USA, securing employment at a dermatology clinic in Los Angeles with the help of a friend. She was giving up her position at the clinic to start a private practice, so it worked out beautifully for everyone. After six months abroad, I needed a job.

I also had to start studying for my certification boards in dermatology. A friend, who had finished a year before me, was also studying for the same exam, and lived nearby. It was helpful to have a buddy, because it was a tough exam. I was juggling three things: studying for the boards, working and studying German.

Karsten and I had a tearful separation in Nepal, but he promised me that he would spend his vacation in the USA during the upcoming summer.

Karsten wrote January 3, 1973:

My dear Joanie,

It is Tuesday evening and you are still in Kathmandu. I don't know how long my letter will take to get to Los Angeles and I want you to have a letter from me when you arrive there.

Have many thanks for the letter from Kathmandu. I was very glad and happy to hear from you. I will send you many kisses as thanks for the nice calendar. I have never before had such a nice calendar.

I was very sad at the Bhairawa Airport as you stepped in the plane and as it flew away. I was standing at the airfield and it was hard to believe that my best friend, "Goldschatz", and hope will be away. I am very thankful for your love, understanding, help and patience, especially with my English. I am thankful for the lovely community we shared together while you were here.

Now I am alone and notice what importance you are for me. I love you very much. My heart is very sad when I think about the time we will be apart.

How was your time in Kathmandu with the Blaskeys and other friends? I hope you will have a nice journey back, my world traveler! Tell me a little about what you see.

Yesterday evening Mr. Berger was visiting me. I invited him for dinner and we had some good conversation until almost 10 PM. He is a very nice man. The day before Hari and a friend came by and we visited until almost midnight. I am very glad to have visitors who speak good English. It is a good exercise for me.

I send you my deep love and many kisses,
Your, Karsten

I wrote on January 20, 1973:

My dearest Karsten,
It was so sad to leave you at the Bhairawa Airport—even now as I think of parting, tears come to my eyes. I miss you and love you very much. Thank you for being so nice to me during my visits. It was such a joy to be with you and already I look forward to our reunion.

The flight back to Kathmandu was smooth and guess who sat by me? Dr. Michaels. He was polite and we had a pleasant conversation. Perhaps I judged his "cold look" in Pokhara too harshly. We all make snap judgments. Anyway, the Blaskeys and I are invited for dinner at their house on Tuesday.

Today Mrs. Blaskey had Sharon and Roger and a Czechoslovakian couple to lunch. It was very nice but I ate too much! Monday I plan to shop with Sharon and hope to get the things on your list. Sorry they will not be in Monday's mailbag, but you should have them on Friday.

I love you so very much. It took me half an hour to compose myself on the flight after I left you. I was crying and Dr. Michaels politely said nothing for which I was grateful.

Hugs and kisses,
Joanie

Dear Joanie,
Since I wrote you last Sunday I received three letters from you. On Monday I got with the mailbag the writing pad and the other things, as well as a short, nice letter. I am very glad and happy that I have you and that you share your feelings. I love you very much, Joanie, and I miss you so much. I pray always for you and us, that God will guide us and give us confidence in our future and Him. I am very thankful that we found each other. . . . . I am starting a wood sculpture for you and I hope you will like it.

Your darling,
Karsten

Karsten like all Europeans was given a generous vacation and he planned to spend at least five weeks in the USA. It would mean five months of being separated. There were many letters written during this time; we wrote each other two to three times a week—no Internet or Skype in those days.

After many months of study, work, and writing letters, our plans of vacationing together in the States became a reality. We decided Karsten would arrive the day before my birthday in June; we would celebrate in New York City! I had already received a letter from the American Board of Dermatology that I had passed the written portion. This was a big relief for me and being with Karsten really would make this milestone, a joyous celebration. The board was given in two parts, so I still had to take an oral exam with professors quizzing me about actual patients. This would take place in October.

Karsten and I fell into each other's arms when we met in NYC at the John F. Kennedy Airport. Meeting someone in those days without a cellular phone seems like a miracle. Wanting to do something special, we went to the Playboy Club and had dinner served by buxom ladies with bunny tails—such were the days!

After a few days, we traveled to Maine. I had fallen in love with Maine one summer, when my friend, Millicent, and I had taken a road trip through New England; I wanted to share its beauty with him. Maine with its rocky coastline and Acadia National Park did not disappoint us. We also visited some mutual friends, a doctor and his wife, who had been in Nepal, volunteering as I had done. They were gracious to us. We eventually made our way back to Boston in our rented car, flying from there to Los Angeles, California, where I had a small apartment.

Not having much vacation time, I continued to work several days a week. We still managed to see San Francisco and other parts of northern California on the weekends. When the five weeks were almost up, we flew back to Philadelphia, where many of my friends, especially Millicent, Pastor and Mrs. Haines, still lived. We announced our engagement! Sticking to the German tradition, we had engagement photo cards printed to send to family and friends. We were able to finalize the prints prior to Karsten's leaving California. We wanted to have them to send to his relatives in Germany. What a dashing couple! Karsten stayed with my former pastor and his wife, while I stayed with Millicent, catching up on old friends and reminiscing. Naturally, we wanted to share this happy event with friends that meant so much to me.

After our visit, Millicent wrote a beautiful letter:

> *Karsten, I want to thank you so much for the two lovely pieces I found on my table—the elephants. I shall treasure them because they are beautiful, and also because I KNOW what great lengths you went to, in bringing them over when you are so limited as to space and weight. Everyone who met you had good things to say about you, and I hope you will take home some favorable impressions of Joan's "Philadelphia family."*
>
> *The Philadelphia family was such an important part of my support system and indeed became better than family!*

Karsten and I hated to say good-bye, but I still had to take Part II of my boards, and he still had a year to fulfill on his contract at the Butwal Technical Institute. It was another tearful separation. I returned to California to work and continue to study.

The letters went back and forth from the USA to faraway Nepal. We wrote several times a week to each other, as we had done before.

In October of 1973, I took the second part of the boards and was feeling so confident, I asked the professor in charge,

"I am engaged to be married, and if I pass the boards, I would like to use my new name, Dr. Joan Gottlieb".

"No problem," was his reply.

My intuition was right and I did pass; the goal of certification had been fulfilled, so I could concentrate more fully on personal matters. After attending the American Academy of Dermatology's annual meeting in December, I flew from San Francisco to Nepal to join Karsten. We had planned to have our wedding the middle of December in the Kathmandu Valley. We had made some friends at the United Mission the previous year, and many were still there. It was such a long distance from the USA and from Germany that it was not possible for any of his family or my friends to join us.

Sharon and Roger were with the British Consul and we had become close. I asked her to be my matron of honor and brought along a dress for her to wear. It had a sweet, multicolored pastel bodice with a blue ribbon sash and a pale pink skirt. Another friend, Patty, fashioned a bridal bouquet out of some roses from her garden and made a cute boutonniere for Karsten's lapel. For myself, I chose a simple white jersey floor length dress with a gathered bodice. It packed well and did not wrinkle. Everyone remarked about how pretty and practical it was. We were married in the Protestant Congregational Church by a friend of the Blaskeys. As loving and generous as the Blaskeys had been to me, it would have been too much to expect them to be there. Serendipitously, they were in the States for the birth of their grandson.

We wrote our own vows and they included some recitations from Saint Francis of Assisi whom we both greatly admired. After the ceremony, we had a light lunch and our wedding cake on the rooftop garden of the Crystal Hotel. The rooftop garden overlooked the Kathmandu valley and we had the good fortune to have a crisp clear day for our celebration.

We had spent most of Karsten's vacation time in the USA, so we did not take much time off after the wedding. Instead, we planned to take five weeks at the end of his contract returning to Germany via southern India, Sri Lanka, and Afghanistan.

In January, we received visitors from Germany; his sister, Frida from Munich and his brother, Franz, a Methodist minister, joined us in Nepal. They were such warm, friendly folks, who made me feel I was truly one of them. It was good that they both spoke English, because at this time my German was very basic.

Franz could not believe how much time it took to prepare meals. Cooking on a wood stove was time consuming and all our water still had to be boiled. Shopping was practically an all day endeavor. I had to walk to the bazaar for fruits and vegetables, but spared myself the sights and smells of the meat market by purchasing buffalo and pork from a woman who delivered a few selections to the house. We had an electric burner, which was used occasionally to warm food or heat water for coffee or tea; but for the most part, the woodstove was where most meals were prepared. Compared to the average Nepali, we were living a most luxurious life.

One of our friends found me a cleaning lady, called Laxmi, named after the Hindu goddess of the same name. This was a common name for girls. Laxmi mainly washed dishes and scrubbed pots and pans. She was a tiny little girl who was so grateful to have a job. Such household work was easy, compared to sitting and crushing stones with a mallet. One often saw many women sitting beside the road, doing these menial tasks for very little pay.

At the Crossroads: A Southern Daughter's Story

Franz only took two weeks vacation and we made several trips in the mountains with him and Frida. On one trip we went to Pokhara and stayed overnight at the Fishtail Hotel. Karsten and his shop had built all the furniture for the hotel; it was situated on a beautiful lake with breathtaking views of the Himalayas. Another time we went to the Tibetan/Chinese border. At this time China was still a closed country. I had time to become acquainted with his brother and sister. We talked about my past and what had happened to me in Georgia. It was a sad story with no really good answers. They were sympathetic.

Karsten's sister, Frida, had saved up extra vacation time, staying almost four weeks at our home. She was able to join us for a short trip to Delhi and Agra. Some of our other friends from the mission decided to come along. It was nice for Frida to have other travel companions, besides her brother and sister-in-law. In Agra, the Mughal emperor, Shah Jahah had built the Taj Mahal, in memory of his beloved wife, Mumtaz Mahal. The Taj Mahal is breathtakingly beautiful. This trip was a wonderful way of affirming our love for each other. We were young and adventurous with unlimited energy!

Karsten and I would be finishing up in Nepal in May and had gotten tips from various people about what to see in Sri Lanka, Southern India, and Afghanistan. We planned to travel four or five weeks in our globetrotting.

Almost everywhere we planned to visit, we had the names of several guesthouses, which provided bed and breakfast at a reasonable price. And it never hurts to have a bit of luck or a guardian angel when you travel; this was certainly true in our case. When we got to Sri Lanka, we found that the trains were on strike. Lucky for us, as we were taking the bus into the heart of Colombo, we spotted a man with socks and sandals getting on our bus.

I said to Karsten, "He is from Germany."

We struck up a conversation with him and sure enough, he confirmed Germany was his home country. Wearing socks with sandals was a common practice in the European community because the climate is cooler. We introduced ourselves. Heinz had been doing development work, teaching repair of farm equipment in Sri Lanka, and was taking one last tour around the Sri Lanka before returning home. He invited us to join him in his VW bug. It was an unbelievable stroke of providence. We went to places we never would have discovered without his expertise. Heinz had been there for three years, learning his way around this area. We visited tea plantations, botanical gardens, the jungle and the coast near the town of Galle. I had never seen pepper trees, camphor trees, cassia (cinnamon), or nutmeg trees. It was so educational and was one of the most fantastic times of our lives. We were going with the flow of life.

We flew back to Madras and made some sightseeing day trips before flying to Bombay (Mumbai) where we also spent more time. Altogether we must have been in India for at least a week. It was so much more congested than Sri Lanka, plus we did not have our personal taxi service anymore. We missed Heinz.

We flew from Bombay to Kabul and stayed at a recommended hotel. A friend of ours had told us to go to the official tourist office and put our names down to share rides to the Bamiyan Valley, about 140 miles west of Kabul. Another stoke of luck happened; a German pastor answered our request and offered to share the ride with us. He and Karsten had become acquainted on a visit to the United Mission. Our guardian angel was really looking out for us.

This valley lay at an altitude of 2500 feet and was a green oasis at the foot of the Hindu Kush mountain range. The three of us stayed in a modest hotel, but we could have gone for the yurts, which are round tents and common to the area. Culturally, it was part of the old Silk Route during the 6th to

At the Crossroads: A Southern Daughter's Story

10th centuries and the crossroads of the cultural exchanges among India, Greece, Rome and Islamic empires. Carved into the Bamiyan Cliffs were two niches, which housed giant standing Buddha statues (165 feet and 114 feet). These statues dated back to the 6th to 8th centuries CE according to some scholars. We were glad our friends had recommended this site to us. The statues were magnificent to behold and we gained access for an even closer look by climbing around the side of the cliff. Regrettably, the Taliban destroyed these beautiful iconic religious works of art in 2001, a desecration that shook the cultured world. Any effort to rebuild them has met with resistance due to the continued war in Afghanistan.

The next evening we visited with our fellow traveler, the German pastor, who had joined us in Kabul, chatting well into the evening. His wife was pregnant and was not able to join him for such exotic journeys. Our modest hotel was comfortable and we had saved money by not succumbing to the expensive yurt, which were more intriguing to the tourists. The next day would be a dusty trip, on unpaved roads, for our visit to the limestone lakes, which lay another 100 miles farther into the Bamiyan Province. Our driver estimated it would take at least two hours to arrive at our destination, the Band e Amir lakes.

The Band e Amir Lakes did not disappoint us. We had never seen such deep blue water; the six interlocking lakes were like simmering sapphires. Formed from limestone, the lakes are separated by natural dams made of travertine, a mineral deposit. With the surrounding hills the color of white sand, and the blue sky overhead, the lakes are truly one of the natural wonders of the world. Recently, in spite of the war, Band e Amir has been named a National Park. Karsten had his bathing suit and took a swim. He said the water was freezing cold, but he had the privilege of saying, "I swam in the Band-e-Amir lakes!"

After the lakes, it was hard to impress us, but we traveled by public bus to the Russian border to a town in the north called Kunduz. Among other things, it was known for its Persian lamb fur products and its colorful headdresses for horse drawn carts. On the way we also went to Mazar-i-Sharif with its famous blue mosque. I remember them as sleepy little towns in 1973, but they were much in the news in 2001. During the Afghanistan war, there was a great siege and battle with the Taliban. It is hard to believe so much has happened in the peaceful world we knew back then.

Karsten enjoyed telling the story of how he was given advice by an older Afghani. The man made motions to him that he should cover my face with a burka. Conservatively dressed in slacks, long sleeves, and a bandana, I had started a conversation with a young man sitting across from me. In retrospect, such actions must have been shocking for the older natives. Thinking at the time, it was a bit of a joke, but came to realize the seriousness of his advice and what it means for women to be required to wear the covering.

We did some shopping but not without assistance. In Kabul, we had this young Afghani, who went everywhere we traveled. He was a great help in purchasing a rug. He may have been spying on us or thought we were spies. We were there the year after the king had abdicated and there probably was more unrest and uneasiness than we realized. How lucky we were to have those guardian angels wherever we went. I sometimes thought that Benton continued to be a guardian angel.

We arrived in Germany to a big fanfare from all of Karsten's family. A big banner had been printed and there were bouquets of flowers from so many people. Now it was my turn to get acquainted with my new family. Almost immediately, I fell in love with Germany and the German people.

At the Crossroads: A Southern Daughter's Story

My mother-in-law was my best German teacher. Cultural immersion is the best way to learn a foreign tongue, but German is a difficult language and has been a lifelong endeavor. My German family has been patient with me and I continue my language studies to this day.

After my tragedy, I voraciously read books by theologians and philosophers searching for meaning. In each book, there was always a golden nugget for me, reading about other people's struggles for purpose in life. The authors, who impressed me the most at this time of my life were Viktor Frankl (*Man's Search for Meaning*), Rollo May (*Love and Will*), Erich Fromm (*The Art of Loving*) and Dag Hammarskjöld (*Markings*). These readings brought me a certain measure of peace and understanding. As did, Paul Tillich, who said in his book, *The Courage to Be*:

> *Life willing to surpass itself, is the good life, and the good life is the courageous life.*

I had been willing to lose myself and in the process had found myself. We learn from experience that there is no final security. Life demands frequently that we surrender security for the sake of self-affirmation. I had not, as they say, "Played it safe." My life had turned into quite an adventure. Karsten had given me a new life with much joy; he had made my tragic loss, history. We both had a lot to be thankful for.

Markings, which was Dag Hammarskjold's diary, was very inspirational to me. He was a Swedish diplomat and former Secretary General of the United Nations and had maintained a spiritual diary throughout his life; this book was published after his death. He summed up my journey when he said:

Jean Gotlieb Bradley

The longest journey is the journey inwards, of him who has chosen his destiny, and has started upon his quest for the source of his being.

What a journey it has been, as it continues to be. I had challenged myself, reached out to the world, and came away a richer person. I try to continue to live with a sense of adventure.

Epilogue

Joan never saw her father again after October 25th 1970. Although Ray died from a heart attack in 1982, he had been hospitalized for arsenic poisoning a few years before. When he asked for a picture of her and her family, Joan sent him a photograph through an uncle. However, Joan's family did not go to his funeral because Karsten felt it would be like saying that her father had no part in the tragic event. Even so, Joan sent a spray of red roses for his casket and grieved for what they might have had.

Karsten and Joan re-established contact with her mother in 1989. In addition to her mental illness, she was becoming old, feeble, and unable to find people who had any patience for her. The sheriff and her lawyer agreed that someone had to intervene. Joan's brother, Johnny, could not manage the situation, but did retrieve their mother from a temporary senior care center in Florida, where the police placed her after she had driven herself there and became lost. Johnny brought her back to Georgia to the local county hospital, where she was hospitalized.

Karsten and Joan met with her doctor and brought Beatrice back to Pennsylvania, where she lived out the remainder of her days. Prior to settling in, she was confined to the West Penn Psychiatric Center for detoxification from all the prescription medicines she had been taking. She went into the DT's (delirium and tremors). When the psychiatrist asked Joan what outcome she expected, she responded quickly with "I want her to be able to dress and feed herself."

After Beatrice was stabilized, she lived a comfortable ten years in an assisted living facility located about thirty minutes from where they lived. Joan wanted her children to have some recollections of their grandmother and often took them along on her visits, so they might know her.

Johnny and Joan never were able to bridge the gap after the tragedy because he thought he had good parents. Later, he had his own set of problems; he married three times and had three children. Johnny became a long distance truck driver, but he never managed to visit their mother, who lived only a short distance from Interstate 70, a route he traveled frequently. Karsten advised Joan against trying to establish more contact because he knew she had enough emotional baggage of her own without adding those of Johnny's.

Joan and her family remained in close contact with the Blaskeys, telephoning them regularly. They always exchanged unique Christmas gifts that remained conversation pieces throughout the years. Living in a Christian retirement community in California, the Blaskeys frequented yard sales and over the years found wonderful books for her two boys. They always inscribed the books from Grannie and Granddad.

The Blaskeys lived well into their 90's; Mavis died of a massive stroke, and John developed Parkinson's disease and died within a year of her death. They were incredible people, as was Anna, their daughter. Joan will always be grateful they enriched her life beyond measure by being a part of her loving and caring family.